Leg Man

Leg Man

Canon

Doyle

NEW PULP PRESS

Published by New Pulp Press, LLC, 926 Truman Avenue, Key West, Florida 33040, USA.

Leg Man copyright © 2016 by Gary Keady. Electronic compilation/ paperback edition copyright © 2016 by New Pulp Press, LLC.

For information contact:
Publisher@NewPulpPress.com

ISBN-13: 978-1945734045 (New Pulp Press)
ISBN-10: 1945734043

Printed in the United States of America
Visit us on the web at www.newpulppress.com

Leg Man

CHAPTER
ONE

Sometimes being a private detective is about as boring as watching the grass grow, not that I can see any grass from my office window. But right now I'm listening to the rain drumming an irritating out-of-time tune on the window at my back. I like my sixth-floor office in downtown Sydney, well, I say downtown but what I really mean is Chinatown – the only affordable office space for a guy with the regular income of a session musician – never knowing when the next paid gig will turn up. I'd been reminiscing the last case and the beautiful Lovejoy twins. The fee had filled the coffers for a while but I still needed to stay frugal in order to survive. It had been a successful mission in the Philippines but a downer coming home to find my message bank with an empty vault. Underneath the stack of unpaid bills on my desk my smartphone, sporting a new ringtone – *Someday Soon*, one of my favorite songs – was keeping noticeably silent. I was willing it to ring when I heard the door of my unmanned reception open.

"Come in!" I yelled out loud enough to reach whoever it was. "My secretary is on holiday." I lied.

The office door slowly opened and a Chinese chick

probably in her mid twenties poked her head in.

"Yes," I said hoping she was a paying proposition.

She pushed the door wide open. No stunner, but sexy, nice legs, bob cut black hair, button breasts – a good figure but wearing a sour look on her dial like someone had just swiped her lunch money. Her demeanor changed to friendly once she'd fixed her eyes on me. My charming looks often have that affect on women.

"So sorry for the interruption," she said apologetically. "Are you detective Stone?"

"You got it Miss ... Axis Stone," I slid my feet off my desk trying to present of more professional image. "Sit down Miss, how can I help you?"

She smiled – nice teeth ... demure, exotic ... maybe even intelligent – wearing no rings and dressed smart casual just short of being designer gear but nevertheless up-market hip – she obviously had a buck – enough to raise my interest anyhow. Just looking at her made my blood ferment and took the chill out of the aircon quicker than a short circuit.

"My name is Jazz Sun ... yes I know, It's an odd name ... my father was expecting a boy," she mused with an angelic smile. "Mr. Stone, my father has a very big problem and it is making him sick."

She looked like she was about to burst into tears, so I jumped up like every practicing gentleman should, and snatched a tissue from the box on my desk.

"Here," I said, handing it to her. I sat on the edge of the desk with a concerned face and my arms folded. "Tell me the problem."

"My father owns the Golden Dragon Restaurant."

"Yeah, I know it ... It's just round the corner. I've eaten

there a few times, nice Gow Gees, good take-away."

"Thank you," she said with a sniffle and then elegantly crossed her legs. Her shapely bare legs and sandaled feet sent my head reeling – it had been a while. I was surprised that my gawking at her pins didn't bother her.

"The restaurant business is very cut-throat Mr. Stone, especially here in Chinatown."

"Call me Axis ... Go on."

"Did you hear about the shark at Manly Beach last month?"

"No, I've been on a job in the Philippines. How does it concern you?"

"Two fishermen were off Long Reef when they hooked a fish, a big fish – a three meter tiger shark. When they hauled it on board it threw up chunks of the burly they'd been using to attract it."

"Lovely, I haven't had breakfast yet so go easy on the gore."

"Well, it also threw up more than the burly Mr. Stone, it threw up a leg ... a human leg."

"So, the police went looking for a man with one leg?" I quipped.

"No Mr. Stone, when my father saw the leg on the news he recognized it."

"Let me get this straight, your father recognized a human leg that had been in a sharks guts for goodness knows how long?"

"Yes, by the tattoo on the ankle."

"Ah ha, so he recognized a tattoo on the leg?"

"Yes, the mark of the fourteen karat."

"You've lost me – the fourteen karat you say?"

"A Triad gang from Hong Kong."

"Okay ..." I mumbled, trying to get a handle on what she was talking about. "And that gang ...?"

"My father's younger brother Chiang is a member or was a member, not sure which."

"So...?" I put forward.

"He went missing after my father received a death threat."

"And why would someone threaten your father?"

"Because he won't sell them the restaurant."

I got up and paced the office floor thinking out loud. "So you think this leg thrown up by the shark belongs to Chiang, and that somebody carried out the threat by using him as burly?"

She began to sob and I realized I was being too flippant when talking about the possible death of her uncle. I put my hand gently on her shoulder.

"I'm sorry, I shouldn't be so insensitive, forgive me."

She blew her nose and frowned, "It's all right Mr. Stone. I understand your vernacular."

I moved in back of my desk and flopped into my high-back swivel chair. It creaked and groaned in protest.

"So what do you want from me Miss Sun? You know the shark leg bit is a police matter?"

"They are pursuing a different line of enquiry Mr. Stone, they haven't made the connection with the Triads and we have no desire to help them."

"Why not?"

"Because the threat still stands, only now they have demonstrated their intent."

"Do you know the identity of the blackmailer?"

"No."

"Does you father?"

"I don't know," she answered sharply.

"Does you father know you have contacted me?"

"No."

"Then what do you expect of me?"

"I want you to find out if it was Chiang's leg, and if it was, who killed him. Then I want you to kill him."

"I'm not a gun for hire Miss Sun ... I don't kill people. Look, at a guess the blackmailer and the killers would probably be Chinese, am I right?"

"More than likely."

"Well, I have no experience in dealing with Chinese."

"Did you have experience in dealing with Filipino's?"

"No, but I sure do now."

"I rest my case," she said and handed me an envelope. There was three grand in crispy one hundred dollar bills inside. "There will be an envelope with the same amount each week and a bonus of ten thousand when you solve the case. Will that be sufficient?"

"It'll do. If I take the case how do you want me to proceed?"

"If you don't want the case I will find someone who does," she returned serve with interest.

"All right ... all right ... I'll take it ... so?"

"I will introduce you to my father as my lover. You will disclose your true job. If my father chooses to take you into his confidence once he knows you are a private eye, then so be it, but you won't disclose I have retained your services. You realize if the blackmailer was to learn you were retained then there could be further reprisals."

"Doesn't this put you at risk Miss Sun?"

"Yes, but it is expected of me, though I must never divulge it."

"Cultural huh, the daughter is dispensable but can act honorably on the side. Is that it?"

"Family honor, Mr. Stone," she said getting to her feet. "I will expect a weekly report from you and regular updates ... kept confidential of course. Here is my card my apartment is nearby. Meet me at seven tonight at the Golden Dragon." A frosted gleam of impatience showed in her sapphire eyes for a moment. Her demeanor had changed radically – a dragon lady had replaced the gentle, demure, lady. She held out her hand to shake.

"Thank you Mr. Stone, I hope you're worth the money," she said slowly.

I leaned over the desk, took hold of her silky, pale, thin hand with perfectly manicured long red lacquered fingernails and locked eyes with her.

"I generally provide satisfaction, Miss Sun."

Her lips twisted in a bad imitation of a smile. She got the sexual innuendo and with a smug glare withdrew her hand. In the blink of an eye she was gone and I was left with a new case to solve. I pushed back in my chair staring at the fat envelope on the desk, happy with myself. I checked my Mac, it was just after midday, time for some research.

~ ~ ~

When I next checked the time it was six thirty, I'd have to freshen up soon to meet Miss Sun and her father. My research of newspapers and a police database that I was fortunate enough to have the key for, had produce results. I now had a clear picture from the police perspective of the shark leg case. I needed to make a moral of it and called my buddy and mentor DI Rick Malone at homicide. He ran it up on his computer but had little to add. The case was going cold, there were no leads on the identity of the leg and few clues from forensics other than that it had been severed by a chain saw. Without any fingerprints it was a dead end and the DNA had yielded nothing because there wasn't a large enough Genomic library in the country yet.

Rick asked what had sparked my interest in the case. I didn't want to lie so I told him a client with a missing relative wanted me to make some subtle enquiries. He suggested I get a DNA sample of the missing person and he would check if it matched the severed leg. I thanked him for the lead and promised to reciprocate should I turn up anything of value.

For emergencies I kept a brand new white dress shirt still in its plastic wrapper in the bottom drawer of my desk along with an electric shaver, a bottle of Davidoff Cool Water eau de toilette, a stick of L'Occitane aluminum free underarm, a tub of VO5 styling wax and a bottle of mouthwash – all a guy needed to get spruced up for a date. I'd just finish admiring my work in the wall mirror when I heard the outside door open.

"Someone there?" I bellowed.

"I'm looking for Axis Stone," the baritone voice replied instantly.

"You've found him. What can I do for you?"

He was a stocky Asian but built like a beach ball, so you didn't notice the height the same way. You could easily think his body was all blubber, and not realize there was only a layer of puppyfat across the powerful muscular tissues. He pulled a blackjack from his inside jacket pocket and slapped it into his palm.

"Sit down," he threatened.

I got the demonstration and obliged him by sitting in the nearest chair.

"Look, if this about someone's daughter I'm sorry, I won't do it again."

There was no sound at all only a sudden shattering pain as the blackjack bounced off the top of my skull, and the dancing plunge into oblivion.

When the pounding pain inside my head had gotten vicious enough to force my eyes open, I found I was draped across the desk like a bundle of last week's laundry. I gripped the edge of the desk hard with both hands and slowly levered myself into an upright position, then swiveled my head around an inch at a time. Fatso had gone but had left a calling card on the chair I'd been sitting on. Unsteady on my feet, I felt the egg sized lump on my head and picked up the card. It had the words *Sun Yee On* typewritten in English with Chinese symbols underneath. I dug around in my desk and found some painkillers. I hadn't been hit by a blackjack before and boy didn't it leave behind a capital headache. It became obvious to me why Vincent Van Gough hacked off his ear, I reckon he had tinnitus and it was driving him nuts, because my left ear was ringing so loud after the whack on the head, that I felt like I'd just come out of a Metallica concert. I was running late – I pocketed the card, snatched my jacket off the hook on the back of the door and rushed out headed for the Golden Dragon rendezvous with Jazz Sun.

CHAPTER
TWO

It didn't make it any easier having to run through rain dodging umbrellas like a rugby player. I arrived at the restaurant puffing, wet and with a 15K tinnitus tone still blasting my left eardrum. A quick scan of the restaurant crowd failed to reveal Jazz. I sighted a sweet-faced Chinese girl behind the reception desk at the entrance, who gave me just a smidgen more than a welcoming smile when I approached her.

"Good evening, sir," she said softly, her face framed by the black lunatic fringe of her bob hairstyle.

"Hi, I'm looking for Miss Jazz Sun."

"Ah yes, you must be Mr. Stone," she punctuated with a sexy smile.

"What's your name honey?"

"Rosy Tong."

"Tong and Stone?" I shook my head. "Nar, they just don't go together do they? We'd never make a Vaudeville act."

She blushed. "Take the door on the left at the back of the room. Miss Sun is waiting for you there."

"Can I have it gift wrapped?" I said briskly.

The corners of her delicate mouth twitched momentarily. "Stone and Tong?" She suggested sweetly.

I figured the desperate run in the rain and knock on the head hadn't affected my sex appeal, so I fired her a wink with my best Mike Hammer ham up.

I swaggered down to the rear of the restaurant and entered the private room.

There were Chinese paintings on blood red wallpaper, red and gold paper ball lanterns and a large single circular table at which was seated a stunning looking woman dressed in a black floral emblazoned cheongsam.

"So nice of you to come Mr. Stone," she said in contralto voice.

"I apologize for being late Miss Sun but I had a visitor," I said handing her the calling card that had be left behind.

Taking it she casually motioned for me to sit beside her. The table was set for six.

"And what did your visitor have to say?"

I took her hand and rubbed her fingers on the lump on the back of my head. "Nothing, he just left this relic along with the card and a whistling left ear."

She retracted her hand like it had been bitten.

"My goodness, why?" she said trying hard to appear genuinely concerned.

""Maybe you should tell me? So who or what is Sun Yee On? If I didn't know better I'd think he was a relative of yours."

"Sun Yee On has nothing to do with my surname Mr. Stone."

"Don't you think you better drop the mister if you're

going to introduce me to your father as your boyfriend?"

"Yes Axis, you're right," she put her hand on my knee like it was supposed to show affection.

Just then the door opened and three Chinese men entered all dressed in suits. The oldest of them approached while the other two stayed by the door. I assumed the old guy was Mr. Sun so I stood to greet him. He sat down without even acknowledging my existence. I stayed standing.

"I assume you're Mr. Sun, my name is Axis Stone."

He motioned dismissively with his hand for me to sit and then spoke in Cantonese to Jazz. Both of them carried on a discussion that sounded more like an argument. Eventually they stopped.

"Is everything all right?" I asked Jazz.

"We were just discussing what to order."

She had me fooled, looked more like they were fighting over the bill. A nod from old Mr. Sun and one of the henchmen slipped out and then returned with two waiters. The first topped up the glasses on the table with water. The other one took the order from Mr. Sun, which sounded more like a demand. They both bowed and scraped backing out of the room like he was royalty.

"You eat anything Mr. Stone?" Sun said with a gruff tone.

"As long as it's cooked and smells good ... I don't like stinking dried fish or offal. Tried some in Manila last month and I'm still getting over it."

He chuckled silently to himself, wasn't sure what to make of that.

"So you two are going out together? Where did you

11

meet and what do you do for a living?"

"We met on the street father, we both live nearby and Axis has an office in the Lee Kung Building," Jazz said politely.

"I'm a licensed private investigator Mr. Sun," I added.

"Does that mean you spy on cheating husband's or cheating wives?"

"Both, but I prefer to avoid that type of work, mostly it's detective work, finding missing persons, researching information, bodyguard work, mostly catching the crooks the police have given up on – to put it in one – it's not what the police look for it's what they miss that I uncover."

"Hmm, sounds like your motto. How long have you been doing this?"

"Worked for three years in an international private detective firm and then branched out of my ace five years ago. I've stayed alive, so that means I'm good at what I do."

"Do you make money Mr. Stone? My daughter is high maintenance you know?"

"I can't say that it provides the regular income you would get from a joint like this but every now and then I pick up windfall."

The door opened and three waiters dressed like chefs entered carrying an array of dishes. First was soup that a waiter ladled from a large bowl into smaller bowls he then placed in front of us.

"The specialty of the house Mr. Stone ... shark fin soup."

I took a taste. "Hmm, puts a different spin on man eating shark," I joked.

Again he chortled silently and then said: "I like your sense of humor Mr. Stone."

Again he and Jazz opened a discussion in Cantonese and this time it sounded even more ferocious. When a pregnant pause came I spoke up.

"Nice soup, no leg in it is there?" I said eyeballing Mr. Sun with intent.

His facial expression changed to dour. With a flick of his index finger he dismissed Jazz. She fired a scowling glare at me before obediently leaving the room.

Mr. Sun patted his lips gently with a napkin, eyeballed me and then growled, "Are you fucking my daughter Mr. Stone?"

"Not yet," I said arrogance free.

Again he flicked his finger and this time it attracted one of his goons who glided over to us like a moth to a flame, drew a blade and held it at my throat.

"Whoa," I yelped and froze.

"I don't like white guys fucking with my family," Sun snarled.

"Maybe that's something you should take up with your daughter, now get this goon to back off or I'll blow his fucking nuts off."

The big bald goon looked down at the .38 I had aimed at his tackle and tensed up. Old man Sun reclined in his chair with a smirk broke on his crabby face. He flicked a more agitated finger at the goon and he backed off locking his switchblade.

"I could get to like you Stone," Sun admitted.

"Get rid of the bookends with knives and your chances will improve considerably," I said slipping my piece back into my leg holster.

He waved his hand and the goons left the room. Once

they'd gone he produced a pocket flask, unscrewed its top and handed it to me. "I'm not permitted to drink, so this has to stay our little secret."

I took a swig ... it was top shelf brandy.

"I might have a job for you Mr. Stone."

I passed him back the flask, "Let's dispense with the formalities ... call me Axis."

He took a big sip from the flask then let out a satisfied sigh. "Okay Axis, you call me Ty."

While he was hiding the flask in his inside coat pocket, I studied him. He was in his mid to late fifties, regal looking, tall for a Chinese with greying sweptback hair. A thin pleasant face with bushy grey eyebrows that shadowed the take no prisoners glint in his eyes. This was a guy who'd survived the pool halls of life.

"I'd smoke if I was allowed to, seems when you get to my age everything you once enjoyed becomes taboo."

"You mentioned a job?" I queried.

"It would have to be on the sly, no mention of it to Jazz. If she gets word of it you won't get the full fee, do I make myself clear?"

"Only if I take the gig ... go on."

"I assume you already know about the shark leg case otherwise you wouldn't have dropped it so wittingly earlier. You were angling for the job Axis and I don't mind that – there's plenty of me in that sort of thinking. Jazz would have told you about my brother Chiang when she hired you. I didn't buy the boyfriend ruse ... Jazz doesn't have boyfriends just handbags. I educated her well."

I was feeling uneasy in my chair. It felt like I'd been set up but the reason was eluding me.

"Let me get this straight … you were onto our little charade and played along with it, why?"

"Because it suits me and we will keep the charade going should you agree to take the case. The reason for doing so will stay my own until I decide otherwise."

"Go on," I said, intrigued.

"How much is she paying you?"

"Three grand a week and ten on completion."

"Okay, you'll keep getting that and I'll double it."

Things were looking up. I liked this game.

"Before you say any more I got this calling card today along with a sly knockout punch." I flicked him the card. He didn't pick it up. His eyes flashed on it then back at me.

"That's what you're up against Axis."

"Did he or they kill your brother and feed him to the sharks?"

"That's what I'm hiring you to find out. Chiang has been missing before."

"But Jazz said you recognized the tattoo …"

"That could have been tattooed on anyone's leg, just for my benefit."

"Why would someone go to that trouble?"

"Because I've been told to sell out and I won't."

"So is the buyer the number one suspect?" I speculated.

"I don't know who the buyer is."

"Okay, so what do you want me to do?"

"Exactly what Jazz would have asked of you."

"But why pay me all that money to do something you could have done through other channels?"

"Because if I make a move, any move, they will kidnap and kill Jazz. I know that. It is the way of the Triad."

"Look, Jazz said Chiang is a gang member of the 14K, the calling card is from Sun Yee On, I assume an opposition Triad gang – in Hong Kong mind you, not Sydney ... I don't fancy getting caught up in some sort of Chinese gang war. I figure that is exactly why you want a white boy to do your probing?"

"You've got it in one Axis, and you will earn plenty of money if you succeed. You're right, this battle is being fought away from the homeland, but that is how it is with the expansion of China. I was born here my father and mother immigrated in 1946. My brother Chiang went home to find his roots and found them all right, it brought us nothing but trouble. Yes, I suspect Sun Yee On is behind the take over bid ... and I admit I am dealing with an unfamiliar problem. That is why I need you Axis, a Chinaman would not succeed these people would get to his family and sway him. Do you understand?"

"Yes, I came upon similar cultural problems on my last case in the Philippines."

"I know, you came recommended by Nick Vargas from Manila."

"Nick! You should have told me that first up ..."

"You know Asian's don't work that way, everything needs to be a mystery."

"Yeah, and don't I know it ... drives me nuts!"

"Good, then do we have a deal Axis?"

"Sure. Any mate of Nick's is a mate of mine."

"He told me you would say that. How will you proceed?"

"First, I'll need some hair belonging to Chiang, I assume he isn't bald."

"No on the contrary, he has very long hair ... a radical

you know."

"Yeah, I sort of expected that."

"What do you need the hair for?"

"DNA testing, to see if it matches the leg."

"Brilliant, see ... already Nick's recommended PI shows great promise."

"Do you know the man who dreamed up the idea of subways was having a dump at the time?"

This time he laughed out loud.

"Nick also warned me to watch out for your crazy sense of humor!"

CHAPTER
THREE

It was good to be out of the rain, one thing I noticed was the whistling in my ear had finally ceased, glad that was over. I was tempted to phone Nick Vargas in Manila to get the dirty laundry on Ty Sun but decided to put my feet up watch a little TV and chill. The meeting with Ty Sun had been taxing. I didn't get to speak to Jazz again and thought of ringing her but settled on a rye on the rocks instead. With my glass in one hand I removed my leg holster, got up and put my best mate Smith and Wesson Model 10, to bed in the drawer of my bedside table. Then I cruised back into the living room to watch Friday night football. I was enjoying my team the South Sydney Rabbitohs giving the Manly Sea Eagles a hiding, when the intercom sounded.

It was Rosy Tong, the pretty receptionist from the Golden Dragon I'd slipped my card to on the way out along with one of my more seductive raves – it had obviously worked.

"Come on up honey," I purred into the hand-piece hoping she was on a mission to break my draught.

I opened the door to her.

"You look surprised, Axis," she said demurely.

"I guess I shouldn't be."

She looked far better than she had at the restaurant,

sexy – older – more mature.

"I hope I didn't keep you waiting long," she said idly, once she got inside the room. She sat down in the nearest armchair and crossed her legs, abbreviating the outline of the delta beneath her skintight black velvet pants. My eyes hungrily followed the line of her thigh right up to the curve of her left buttock, then when I saw the way she was looking at me, my throat suddenly went dry.

"Didn't you think I would come?" she said seductively.

"Oh, I had my hopes. How about a drink?"

"I'll have whatever you're having," she purred.

"Bourbon," I told her.

"Sure, I haven't tried that before."

"Well, there's a first time for everything honey," I told her as I made the drinks, "it's the finest sour mash you've ever tasted."

She pulled a face. "It sounds like something out of the gutter."

I gave her the drink and she sipped it cautiously first, then drank until the glass was empty.

"I approve," she said carefully, then handed me back the glass. "I think more, please?"

After I'd made her another drink and given it to her, I settled down in the opposite armchair to sip mine. "You know something?" I said slowly. "You fascinate me, Rosy."

"Is that so Axis?" Her mouth twisted sardonically. "But I'm only a receptionist, so what's the attraction?"

"You're sexy."

"Seriously?"

She drank some more bourbon like it was Sprite or something.

"If you're not used to that stuff it can kick like a mule, be careful."

She got up suddenly, carried her glass over to the window, and stood looking out with her back to me.

"Still raining?" I said turning the television off. My team had won anyway.

She turned back and tossed the empty glass into my lap.

"You don't mind if I take my clothes off, do you?" she asked. "It helps me relax."

"Relax as much as you like," I said truthfully.

"But I'll keep my boots on."

"Please yourself," I said putting the remote down on the glass coffee table. I looked up and saw the boots, and Rosy Tong – all of her, standing there with her hands on her hips and, apart from the boots wearing only a provocative smile. I stared at her, and as I did so, I was aware of the slow unfurling of my rod from its customary resting place. Her body was like alabaster, stunning.

"You look surprised, Axis," she said in a soft, husky voice.

"You did say you wanted to relax."

"I sure did," I agreed.

"Relax and make love, Axis." Her smile broadened lewdly, and slowly she ran her hands in from her hips and down her sleek flanks, the tips of her fingers almost touching the dark wiry wedge between her legs.

"What's the matter, Axis? Don't you want me?"

The knee-length black boots contrasted sharply with the whiteness of her skin. Her dark pink nipples were standing erect from their surrounding puckered areoles. Her legs were slightly parted, and the dark hair of her delta tapered to a small tuft between them. The slit of her vulva was almost obscured by the thin strands of black hair that only just covered it, her clitoris protruding, beckoning my lips. I swallowed hard as she walked toward me in a kind of free-swinging symphony, lifted the glass out of my frozen hand, and drained it.

"I hope I am not embarrassing you, Axis," she said looking at me salaciously over the rim of the glass.

"No, no," I yelped.

"Then why don't *you* relax?" Her voice was sensual, and her eyes dropped momentarily to my crotch. "I can see you're keen, so I don't think there's any fear of me being rejected, is there?"

I was conscious of her closeness to me and of the throbbing demands of my swollen prick, which was desperate to escape its suffocating confines. "You're right," I croaked.

"Take your clothes off."

Which is what I did, hurriedly, with fumbling awkward fingers, leaving them on the floor where I had thrown them. I didn't expect her to be so dominant, not this demure little thing. My raging prick reared upwards and out from my pelvis, and she came up to me again, wrapping her arms around me and pressing her body hard against mine, her pelvis gently gyrated against me, I could feel it throbbing against her moist flesh.

Then she was pulling me down onto the floor, easing me onto my back, and as I lay there passively, seeing her body from a entirely new perspective, her swinging small but full breasts, the pink gape of her distended sex, she straddled me, and taking hold of my rod, guided it into the smooth, lubricated warmth of her sheath, which absorbed it right up to the hilt so that her body hair brushed against mine. She began to move over me, her body rising and falling, her vaginal muscles gripping the tip of my rod so that it didn't slip out. Then *Someday Soon* started playing on my smartphone. I reached out a hand and fumbled my discarded pants for the phone to check the ID of the caller. It was Jazz. I had to take it. Rosy kept working me, enjoying me filling her to the max. She was getting off on me taking to the boss's daughter while she was fucking me.

"Hello Jazz, no, it's not a good time right now … I'm up to something I need to finish." It was a massive effort to keep a grip on the conversation with Jazz while Rosy was keeping a grip on me. I could tell by her rapid panting she was coming to a climax … I wanted to join her in the chorus. "Okay," I said hurriedly to Jazz. "The Grind Café (ironic) in Sussex Street at 8 a.m. See you then, bye." And then we both hit the ceiling.

After we'd regained our composure we sat together naked on the three seat lounge. "Well who would think Tong and Stone were going to put on such a great performance?" I said.

"Yes, we make a fine duet."

"Let me take off those boots, I'm a bit of a leg man with a foot fetish."

"Uh uh," she said with a shake of the head and moved her legs away so I couldn't remove the boots. "I need to freshen up, can I use the bathroom?" She stood and little girl like posed with her legs parted so I could see my juice around her wet slit.

"Sure, in through the bedroom."

As she floated off carrying her clothes towards the bedroom I settled back and admired her beautifully rounded butt and hourglass figure. Oh how I'd like to see her without those boots.

She stopped at the door to the bedroom and turned. "Axis, can I ask you something?"

"Sure, babe, anything."

"Why did you have a meeting with Mr. Sun and his daughter?"

"Oh, just a little business."

"Does she turn you on?"

"Who Jazz? Can't say that she does ... no."

"So it's just business then?"

"Are they going to hire you to find Mr. Chiang?"

"I can't discuss the case, honey, I'm sorry."

"Oh, I see," and she disappeared into the darkness.

I heard the shower and was tempted to invade her to give her another one but I knew it was only my foot-fetish kicking in – hide something from Axis and he craves to uncover it – I guess that's the detective in me. I got dressed – the action was over for the evening. I had no doubts she was going to leave or she wouldn't have wanted to freshen up.

I was having breakfast with Jazz in the Grind café, sipping our orange juice companionably like a sedately married couple. She had a fresh glowing look about her as though she was set to take a ten-kilometer jog after breakfast.

"Well, I hope you got done *whoever* or whatever you needed to do last night," she said facetiously.

"Yes as a matter of fact I did."

"We didn't get to speak after dinner at the restaurant."

"No, Daddy gave you the bullet quick smart, is that normal?"

"Business to him is a man's world."

"You don't aspire to that philosophy?"

"I think the world has grown up since the days when women were considered a sub species. Which brings me to the point, did he retain your services?"

"He sure did."

"For the same reasons I retained you?"

"Yep."

"So, do I still have to pay you?"

"If you wish to continue our contract, yes."

"But you have been retained by my father isn't that now a conflict of interest?"

"It was what you asked me to do wasn't it?"

"Yes, I expect you're right. It doesn't matter its all his money anyway. What is your next move then?"

"I need a few locks of Chiang's hair for DNA analysis to see if it matches the shark leg."

"I'll get his girlfriend to drop a brush or something over to me."

"Don't worry, I'll pick it up, I'd like to look over his place for clues anyhow. Is that where he disappeared from?"

"Yes, she was at work ... he was home. She found signs of a fight, things broken."

"Okay, I suppose it's all been cleaned up since so there'd be no point in getting prints, but I still want to check it out."

"When?"

"As soon as."

"Okay, I'll arrange it," she said typing a text on her phone. "I'll text you the address once it's organized – his place is not far from here, a Darling Harbor apartment. There's something else I want you to do."

"Go on," I muttered.

"My father visits Fortune Garden in Surry Hills very often and I think he might owe them money."

"Fortune Garden, isn't that a restaurant?"

"Yes, and a mahjong room, it is *the* place in town for wealthy Cantonese Chinese to gamble."

"Okay, so do you think they might be behind the kidnapping or the take over offer for the Golden Dragon?"

"Maybe, I just know some of his secret habits, and Chinese men of his age do tend to gamble sometimes to the extreme."

"Does he have a wife or a girlfriend or both?"

"My mother died when I was fifteen, I am the only child. My father has had many mistresses but this is what makes me worry Axis, in the last few years he hasn't had one. Something else must be satisfying him, and it can't be work."

"All right, I'll look into it. Tell me, your father said he was recommended to me, and you told me you just heard about me, so what is it?"

"Oh a family friend recommended you. I'm sorry, I should have told you but I didn't know how my father was going to react to you."

"You weren't sure he'd hire a Gweilo?"

"You know the Chinese term for a white guy – Gweilo: green-eyed devil. Ha, we don't use it, we're Australians, but yes, I though he might expect to deal with it himself ... and

I figured that'd be dangerous – he's too old for that sort of shit."

"Is the family friend by chance a Filipino named Nick Vargas?"

She blushed, "Yes, Nick is a distant cousin."

I immediately suspected there was more to it than that by the way her cheeks flushed. I figured she and Nick had a closer relationship than she was intimating. I rocked back in my chair and gave her the once over. Yes, she was Nick's type ... we have similar taste considering we both dated twin sisters Kitty and Lola Lovejoy. Jazz has a similar figure to Kitty and also his ex fiancée Bianca Gutierrez. Wearing a skirt that rode up over her knees offered me a good view of her shapely legs. After the discussion with Rosy last night I was now beginning to change my mind about whether Jazz turned me on or not. Then I noticed her feet. She was wearing sandals that showed off her feet and they were exquisite, probably the best feet I've ever seen. My mouth watered at the thought of sucking her toes and licking her legs.

"Axis, you're staring at my feet."

I looked sharply back at her face like I'd been caught with my pants down.

"Sorry, I was just thinking."

"Thinking about what ... a pedicure?"

"That you have lovely legs and the most beautiful feet I think I've ever seen."

"Thank you, do you have a foot fetish?"

"Yep, naked feet and legs seriously do it for me."

"Well, we have something in common there." Her phone buzzed interrupting the train of thought. She looked at it. "Oh, I have to go. I'll text you about Chiang's apartment. You can pick up the bill seeing you're on such a good stick. Report to me as soon as you have something. Bye."

"What no kiss on the cheek?" I complained. "I am after all supposed to be your boyfriend."

"Not after you've turned yourself on gawking at my feet. This is not the place or the time for that."

I watched her leave believing the context of her parting statement was to leave me on a promise. I figured if Rosy was such a top performer then Jazz might well be a star.

CHAPTER
FOUR

I'd only just entered my office when *Someday Soon* alerted me to a message. It was the address of Chiang's apartment from Jazz. There was no point in beating around the bush I needed the hair follicles for DNA testing so I headed for Darling Harbor. It was only a short walk from the office and the rain had quit – the sun was shining – Sydney smelt fresh and the walk was invigorating. The Shelly Street Apartments Plus complex overlooking Darling Harbor, a stone's throw from the new Barangaroo Casino development, is one of the ritziest in Sydney and would have cost Chiang an arm and a leg – pardon the pun.

I pressed the intercom buzzer for 905, the penthouse, and a small female voice answered.

"Axis Stone … Miss Jazz Sun sent me."

A loud buzz signaled to enter. I'd been in the block before, expensive short stay apartments occupied the first few floors but the remainder was privately owned. A quick ride up in the elevator and I was soon at the double doors of apartment 905 about to knock when they suddenly opened. I was immediately taken aback by who was there to greet me.

"Rosy baby! You're the last I expected!" I exclaimed.

She looked irritated. The boots and get up had gone, she was back to looking demure but grumpy.

"Mr. Stone," she said calmly and then permitted me to enter.

I looked about – it was a huge apartment, probably took up half the floor. Ultra modern in design and decor with a chrome staircase winding creatively up to a mezzanine that probably housed a couple of bedrooms. Everything was white and chrome and designer, right out of Home Beautiful, except there were several large original, ghastly colorful paintings with a distinct Chinese flavor hung on the walls. Rosy sat on the three-seat white leather lounge.

"Fancy pad honey, so are you just minding the fort or part of the furniture?"

"Chiang is my boyfriend," she snapped dispiritedly and hurt.

"So why fuck me last night?"

"Because I'm left out of the loop, the Sun family treats me like trash. I wanted to know what's going on, you were my best bet."

I flopped into the big comfy white soft leather lounge chair opposite her. This time I could see her legs but not her feet sadly she was wearing ankle-high boots.

"So should I feel used and abused?"

"Why not, I do all the time, the feeling shouldn't be reserved just for me."

I scanned the room, "You don't seem to be doing too bad for a receptionist."

"It's an illusion, Axis, one puff and it's all gone, just like Chiang.

"Is it rubber glove or a gold digger thing with you and him?"

"A relationship of convenience for him, a regular fuck that

wasn't going to give him heat and wouldn't be badgering him about marriage because it was below his station."

"A concubine?"

"You could call it that, so no ... definitely not love, just lust, and a better life for a girl from the western suburbs of Sydney whose parents still refuse to speak English after living here for twenty-five years."

"Oh, my heart bleeds for you," I said sarcastically.

I got up. I'm going to take a look around.

"Be my guest," she grumbled.

"Are the bedrooms upstairs?"

"Yes."

I made my way up the chrome staircase and entered the main bedroom. This guy was a dude, he had all the playboy toys – a huge round bed with a massive overhead circular mirror – the walls were all white but the blood red shag pile carpet spelt seduction. Any bird brought here knew what she was in for.

"You might like this," a small voice came from behind me and Rosy pressed a button on the wall. Two chrome chains with black leather wristbands dropped out of a small hatch in the mirror above the bed.

"He liked to chain me up naked, sometimes he'd then go out with his friends and leave me hanging there ... sometimes for days." She pressed another button and a drawer slid silently open at the base of the bed. Laid out inside it like in a shop display was an array of sex toys. Suddenly, the S&M black boots Rosy was wearing last night made more sense.

"His choice of toys," she said flippantly. "The ugly one's for inflicting pain are his favorites."

"He sounds a lovely guy, it's no wonder the shark threw him up."

I checked the bureau.

"I'll need a photograph of Chiang, none on show, got one?"

"He avoids being photographed for some reason, paranoia probably."

"Yeah? Why's that?"

"I don't know, seems he always feels threatened or something. I've got one, I'll just get it."

While she cruised off to get it I went into the walk-in wardrobe, which was almost bigger than my entire apartment.

"He's got more suits than the men's section of Walmart for Christ's sake."

Rosy came back and followed me into the wardrobe.

"Here, that's him on the left earlier this year."

I studied it. There were two guys and three hot Asian chicks posing by a swimming pool. The two guys were archetype Chinese gangsters, dark wrap-a-round shades, dapper suits and ties, while the three girls were in the briefest string bikinis.

"Who's the other guy?"

"No idea," she replied sharply.

"And the chicks?"

"Probably prostitutes, I don't know any of them."

"How come you've got the photo?" I said pocketing it.

"I found it just before he went missing. We had a huge fight over it," she growled.

I slid a large door open, "What about all these ties?"

There must have been a thousand of them all different

colors and patterns and all meticulously rolled up.

"No one would ever get to wear all of them. Does he wear them or just collect them?"

When I didn't get an answer I turned around to find she had split.

After an hour of searching every nook and cranny for a clue, to no avail, I decided to make my way back downstairs. I found Rosy sitting on the lounge sipping a drink. She pointed at a glass waiting for me on the coffee table. I picked it up, took a sip and sat down.

"Hmm, nice drop, vintage Jack?"

"Yes, when Jazz said you were coming over I ordered it in. It's old number seven."

"You've got class my dear," I said sitting down.

"It was quite a night," she said in a purring voice.

"From what I saw upstairs I feel a rank amateur."

"There's a world of difference between lovemaking and whatever Chiang calls it. You make sex a wonderful experience for your partner, but for him, it's all about himself and inflicting pain on others, that's what turns him on."

"So if it was his leg the shark belched up then what happens to all this ... and you for that matter?"

"All gone, me too," she said bitterly.

I downed the drink and then stood ready to leave, "Well, thank you for the drink Rosy, I'd stay and throw a few more down but I've got work to do. Oh," I pulled a hairbrush out my pocket, "I'm taking this for DNA testing, I assume it's his brush and his hair?"

"Yes, it is. When will I see you again?"

"Let's just keep in touch, I'd like that." I turned to leave.

"Axis?" I turned back to her. She had slipped off her shoes so I could see her feet. She stood and lifted her skits up to just below her panties giving me a view of her lovely naked legs and stunning bare feet.

"You're sending me away with a hard on, you know that?"

"Well get it out and bring it here I know just what to do with it."

~ ~ ~

I left the apartment divested of 10 CC of seminal juice Rosy had swallowed. She'd left a glow on my face that could be read like a beacon from a mile away.

I hopped a cab to police HQ in Surry Hills.

~ ~ ~

Detective Rick Malone was in his office typing on his computer when I knocked on the glass door. He motioned with his hand for me to enter.

"Detective Stone, sit down what can I do you for?" He said in his usual devil-may-care manner.

I handed him the brush. "Here tidy yourself up Rick you're a fucking mess." He was just about to brush his hair with it when I growled, "Stop! It might be evidence!"

He froze before it touched his mop of greying medium length unruly brown hair.

"Ah ha! The brush and hair belonging to your missing person."

"Exactly, delivered as promised."

"Oh, you're the height of efficiency young man.'

'Some call it perfectionism, I call it attention to detail.'

'I meant to ask how Manila was, nudge, nudge, wink, wink?" he grinned.

"You mean did I get laid? Yes heaps – was it good,

brilliant – should we go there for a fucking holiday for certain but your wife Judy mightn't agree."

"There's always some stick in the mud isn't there? Oh well, so you got what's-her-name back then?"

"Kitty Lovejoy?"

"Yeah, what a name – the mind boggles."

"What made it worse is she has a twin sister Lola Lovejoy, an even better looker."

"Did you?"

"Client confidentiality doesn't permit me to discuss that in detail but in short, absolutely."

"That's my boy! Now hang fire while I get this off to the lab."

He dialed the phone on his desk and mumbled into the receiver. A couple of seconds later a female police officer in uniform knocked and entered.

"Detective sergeant Parker, this is my good friend Axis Stone, he's a private dick."

In her late twenties her sharp facial features were accentuated by her blonde hair tried neatly back, and her uniform. I could tell by the two bulges in her jacket she was well endowed and I looked down at her stocking legs to check the shape of them – nice.

"Finished the once over Mr. Stone private dick. By the undressing it may not be so private," she jousted.

"New is she?" I asked Malone with a sarcastic smirk.

"Yes, it'll take her a few weeks to settle in. Either she'll sue for gender harassment or she'll fit-in just fine."

"By her attitude I think the latter will be the case mate," I said with a smile.

"Now he's trying to crawl up my ass. Are all your friends

like this chief?" She growled.

"Yep, every one of them," he smiled,

"Good, it's going to be great working here," she said and held out a hand.

We shook hands and boy did she have a strong grip. Rick handed her the hairbrush.

"Can you get this down to forensics sergeant, we need it checked for a DNA match on the shark leg."

"Nice to meet you Axis, I'll catch you round the traps," she said on the way out.

"Sure thing," I bellowed back, and then shot Rick raised eyebrows. "She's a bit of a sort aye?"

"Yeah, half the flying squad have been sniffing around her since she moved here from the south coast."

"No wonder, you rarely get a stunner like that working with you flatfoot's."

"Ain't that so. Anyhow you keep your filthy mitts off-a her, I don't want her soiled by your bad habits."

"How are Judy and the tin lid's?"

"Kids! Cripes, tells you how long it's been since you were around for dinner. The tin lid's have all grown up and left home. Judy's the same, plays golf, cooks wonderful meals and complains about my snoring – such is life. When are you going to settle down?"

"Not cut out for the happy nuclear family routine, mate. Besides, I've not yet met the right bird."

"You've got to get past their vagina to do that Axis, you do realize that don't you?"

"Sure mate, you're always full of great advice and wisdom, that's why I come visit you."

"So to whom does the hair belong?"

"One Chiang Sun."

"Sun ... sun .... hmm, that name rings a bell. We got word on the shark leg case that there might be Triad involvement. The DNA forensics determined the leg belonged to an Asian male probably Chinese."

"Well, there you go, we might just be on to something. You say you've heard of Sun before?"

"Yeah, something to do with a bust a few years back ... now what was it? I know, an illegal mahjong school run by him and other members of his family. Doesn't he own a restaurant?"

"Yep, the Golden Dragon in Dixon Street."

"That's the bloke. Glad the old memory is still ticking," he chuckled. "Vice shut down his little back room casino. He just got a fine, no arrest."

"Speaking of that, have you heard anything about a local restaurant the Fortune Garden being a mahjong school?"

"Rumors, do you want me to check with vice?"

"Why not?"

He picked up the phone, "I'll ask Bill Rogers ... Bill, its Rick Malone, good thanks ... listen, do you have anything on the Fortune Garden ... ah ha, okay ... thanks, I'll let you know if I hear anything. No, cards are on for tomorrow night, see you then, cheers." He put down the phone. "Yes, it's under surveillance for illegal gambling, prostitution and drugs, does that help?"

"It's a real worry that's what it is. How long for the DNA results?"

"Give it a couple of days. I'll call you."

I got up to leave. "Thanks, buddy."

"Watch your back, Axis. These Chinese are something else to deal with."

"You're telling me. They're as confusing as Confucius."

CHAPTER
FIVE

As I left Homicide I realized it was lunchtime and I was feeling a little peckish but before I could do anything about it *Someday Soon* sounded. I answered.

"Stone, yes Ty, I was just thinking about that. Sounds nice, okay I'll be there in about fifteen minutes. Okay bye." I hopped a cab to the Cockle Bay public wharf in Darling Harbor where a Grainger Custom 50 Catamaran was moored at the end of the wharf.

Ty's favorite henchmen let me on board and I found him in the galley sitting at a table in front of a spread of steaming hot Chinese dishes. He wasn't alone there was a man with his back to me.

"Ty, I hope this thing isn't going to move, I promised myself never to step on a boat again after a high-sea adventure that went wrong in the Philippines."

The man stood, turned and faced me, "And a great adventure it was Axis," Nick Vargas said beaming a huge smile.

"Nick, you're a sight for sore eyes!" I said happily.

"Sit down guys, let's eat and talk," Ty said.

"What brings you to Sydney?" I asked Nick.

"I'm on my way to meet Kitty in Brisbane, I was talking to Ty and he threatened I had to call into for a drink, so here

I am. Have you spoken with the Lovejoy's since you got back?"

"No, to be honest I've been too busy," I lied, "and now I've got this case ... thanks for the recommendation by the way."

"I've known the Sun family all my life, happy to help in their hour of need. I went to Oxford with Chiang, you know, we played rugby together," Nick said.

"A long history ... have you spoken with the police about Chiang?" Ty asked me.

"Yes, they confirmed the leg belonged to an Asian but that's about all they've got. I've given them some of Chiang's hair for DNA testing."

"To try and match with the leg?" Nick asked.

"Yes, we should know in a couple of days."

~ ~ ~

After lunch Nick and I took a walk along the wharf.

"Nick, can I speak candidly?"

"Are you asking if what we talk about stays between us? If that's what you wish Axis, yes."

"Okay, tell me what you know about Ty and Chiang."

"Look there's a Starbucks over there let's sit and have a coffee," Nick suggested.

~ ~ ~

After getting a couple of coffees we sat in the alfresco setting under and umbrella.

"Chiang is a wild and crazy guy. They come from old money. It's rumored old man Sun made a lot of money out of World War II, they say from the Japanese."

"Really?"

"Don't quote me on it Axis, it is family myth and not

necessarily fact, but he did immigrate to Australia in 1947 with a shit-load of money and was being hunted by the Communist Party."

"I was told Chiang's a Triad member, would that true?"

"Well, that brings up another myth: was old man Sun the head of the Sun Yee On in Canton and fled with black money because he anticipated Chairman Mao would take power of China in 1949, and form the People's Republic – which he did."

"Either story puts Ty and his family in jeopardy."

"It does, especially when the old man and his wife were murdered here in 1959, then Ty's wife was run down in a hit and run in 2004."

"We're the perps caught?"

"Ty has always maintained there are plants high up in the police or in local government here shielding the killers, just as it happens in Manila, remember Mayor Rodriguez?"

"That reminds me, did you and Mayor Rodriguez have anything to do with the accidental deaths of the murder's of Ringo Raye and Arnel Gutierrez?"

He locked eyes with me, "Let's just say we had an agreement that came to fruition."

It was an admission that he and the sinister Mayor of Makati had conspired, as I had presumed, to have Raye and Gutierrez killed before they would ever go to trial. That did the job of keeping the mayor's name out of the media and closure for Lovejoy family. But it wasn't closure for the family of Ricky Esposo my off-sider shot to death in a drive-by or Chicki Dee an innocent bystander who got her throat cut leaving behind a six year old son with a decrepit old mother and no money or the Cortez family for the loss of

Pablo, an undercover cop on a drug bust, murdered by in cold blood by one of Raye's men.

"With all I know I can't reconcile that Nick, I know it's the Filipino way, but there's too much carnage to brush under the table by letting a crook like Rodriguez walk free."

"I admire your morality Axis, but don't be under the illusion that this case is any different. Ty Sun is nearly broke, Chiang was dabbling in everything from the sex trade to drugs."

"What about the daughter Jazz?"

"I think she's the only good thing about the family."

"Have you bonked her?"

"Yes, but a long time ago. I took her flower. But it was only that once when we were both too young for it to mean anything."

"Can I trust her?"

"Yes, but always remember how thick blood is with the Chinese – they're worse than Filipino's and much, much, more crafty and ... complicated ... so complicated at times that even with my little bit of Chinese blood I get lost in the chaos of their cultural hang-ups."

"I thought you had Spanish blood ..." I said with a chuckle."

"Most Filipino's have a measure of Spanish, Chinese or even Arab running in their veins. Just watch your back my friend, I won't be there to help this time – but I'll only be a phone call away."

"Thanks buddy and look, give the girls a kiss for me. Tell Lola when I get this one done I'll pay her a visit."

I left Starbucks much wiser than I had arrived thanks to Nick taking me into his confidence. But at the same time

I was left with a quandary, who the stuff am I going to trust on this case? The answer was obvious – no one. I headed back to my office to set my traps. On the way I put my hand in my pocket and found the calling card from the Sun Yee On and it suddenly downed on me that I'd seen the Chinese logo on the card somewhere else – on Rosy Tong's ankle. That's why she wouldn't take the boots off last night! She didn't want to expose a link to the Sun Yee On. The revelation only confused me further. I needed to sit in my office with a bottle of Jack and think it all through.

~ ~ ~

I looked at the bottle on my desk through the haze of confusion and thought; *I'd rather have a bottle in front of me than a frontal lobotomy* – then *Someday Soon* announced a caller.

"Jazz, hi, I'm at the office. Nick, yes, I know, I had lunch with him and your father. Yes, I got the hairbrush ... it's with forensics ... a couple of days they said. No, I'm going to Fortune Garden tonight for a snoop. Okay I'll call you then. Bye."

~ ~ ~

I reserved a table at Fortune Garden for 8 p.m., and then rang Rosy to see if she'd like to accompany me – there was no reply so I left a message. It was an upmarket joint so I decided to put on my best casual clobber expecting to hear back from Rosy before leaving – but she didn't call. As a result I headed off to Fortune Garden on my ace. I had thought of asking Jazz to be my date but then reconsidered thinking she might be too recognizable to the local Chinese high rollers I expected to find there.

A taxi dropped me at the entrance to what looked like a

pagoda oddly positioned within a nest of residential terrace houses, typical of Surry Hills. Inside, the Chinese motif grew even more spectacular, had I not known better I could have walked through a time warp and been transported to Hong Kong.

A sweet Chinese lass dressed in a white Cheongsam guided me to a table. She made me realize Rosy and Jazz were special when it comes to Asian sexuality - this one had little. There were few patrons perhaps it was too early. I ordered a JD on the rocks then rocked back in my chair to study the menu. It didn't take long before I noticed Chinese patrons being led to another room at the rear of restaurant and figured it must be the casino. After ordering I called over the maître d.

"I was told I can play mahjong here?"

"I'm sorry, sir, members only," he said emphatically. "Can I get you anything else sir?"

"Just what do you think you've already got me when you ask that? ... Pompous ass." I mumbled the last two words.

"I'm sorry, sir?"

"Just bring me another JD on the rocks," I ordered dismissively.

"Certainly, sir."

After eating I fixed the bill and left, as there was nothing to be gained from sitting in the restaurant watching the clientele. What I needed to see was the gaming rooms.

~ ~ ~

Outside I walked to the end of the block and found a lane that connected to a street behind the restaurant. My days of spying on cheating husbands and two-timing wives put me in good stead to finding a way into the rear of the restaurant and hopefully the casino. In the street behind – sure enough – Bingo! Half a dozen wheelie bins marked FG were lined up right beside a narrow walkway that I knew would lead to the Fortune Garden kitchens. Flanked by three story buildings the alleyway was dark but safe, no one would be expecting me and if I got caught, I'd simply declare I'd taken a wrong turn. As I closed on the rear of the restaurant I could hear music. The lane came to a fork. I deduced by the wheelie bin tracks on the ground that one way led to the kitchens and the other had to be the casino. I followed my instincts and came to a locked door. I put my ear up to it and heard music, voices and glasses clinking. It had to be the casino – then, confirmation – I recognized the sound of mahjong dice being thrown on a table. There must be a window I figured, so I walked to the end of the alleyway looking for one and found a six-foot wooden fence separating the restaurant from the building next door, and one floor up there was a window – probably to a bathroom. If I climbed onto the fence I'd be able to reach it. Rickety as it was I balanced on top of the fence and then reached across to the window with my hand hoping it was open. Jackpot – it opened and was just big enough for me to fit in through. I was right it was a bathroom. The light was out – it was dark but I could see there were three cubicles, three wash basics and a mirror extending the length of the sidewall. With no urinals it was definitely the ladies bathroom. As I started towards the door I heard someone approaching from the other side and so ducked into the nearest cubicle and locked the door. The fluorescent lights flicked on and I could hear two women speaking in Chinese. One of them entered the cubicle beside mine and kept talking while taking a pee. I was hoping the other woman wasn't going to get the urge to do the same. The door handle jiggled with her trying to open it and she babbled something that must have been a Chinese obscenity and went into the next cubicle. The two of them were peeing and chatting and I had no idea what they were talking about. The first one finished, flushed, and then sounded like she was chopping up a couple of lines of cocaine on the toilet cistern. She called the other one in when she'd finished and they tooted the rails. I thought no, now they're going jabber on for the next half hour off their faces – but they didn't – they giggled a bit and left. It was time to make an exit before another encounter so I quickly followed behind them.

I didn't count on being the only Gweilo in the casino, so when I walked into the well lit room I stood out like a sore thumb. I knew it would soon be over for me, so I quickly scanned the gamblers not expecting to see a familiar face.

CHAPTER
SIX

Suddenly, two big bouncers appeared out of nowhere and took one of my arms each ready for the bum's rush out of there.

"You're the last person I expected to see here Nick!" I growled.

He and Ty came over to me.

"Old habits die hard I know Axis but instead of making a private eye entrance, especially through the ladies, all you had to do was ask and we would have brought you along," Nick said calmly.

A quick word in Chinese from Ty and the two goons released me.

"Jazz told you to check if I was gambling didn't she?" Ty muttered so it was kept between us.

"Yes," I acknowledged.

"She probably thinks I'm in debt for millions and that is the source of our problems, correct?"

"Something like that."

"Nick, am I in debt?"

"Not as far as I know Ty."

"Thought you said you were going to Brisbane today?" I snapped at Nick.

He checked his wristwatch, "Sure am, the flight goes at

11.30, Ty promised to get me to the airport on time. It's getting late," he said glancing at Ty.

"Come on let's go, we can talk in the car," Ty said moving off with Nick and myself in tow.

~ ~ ~

We were in the chauffeur driven stretch limo just about to head off to Sydney Domestic Air Terminal to drop Nick off when *Someday Soon* sounded. I drew my phone. There were two texts from Rosy. I opened the most recent it said *905 help*! Knowing she wouldn't send a message like that unless there was real trouble, I tried to ring her but only got a message bank.

"What is it Axis, something wrong?" Nick asked sensing my mood swing.

"A text from Rosy Tong asking for help."

"What the floozy that hangs around Chiang like a bad smell?" Ty said disapprovingly.

I ignored the slur. "You better let me out I need to find out what's wrong. I don't think she'd ring me unless it was serious."

"No way, I hired the limo, where is she?" Nick said genuinely concerned.

"Shelly Street Apartments Plus Darling Harbor," I told the driver through the partially open partition.

"That's Chiang's apartment!" Ty barked.

"Yes, he lives with the floozy!" I said facetiously, like he didn't already know. "The very same floozy that works seven days a week for you as your restaurant receptionist."

"Ah! I don't know half the stuff that's going on right under my nose," he grumbled. "I leave all that public relations crap to Jazz."

"Looks like you'll miss your flight mate," I said to Nick ignoring Ty. I didn't like the air superiority he seemed to express over people.

"No matter, I can get the 6 a.m." He drew his phone. "I'd better call Kitty, she's supposed to pick me up from the airport. " He got her message bank and left an update.

"Want me to ring Lola to make sure?" I asked him.

"No thanks, Kitty will get it, besides you might have some explaining to do if you call Lola," he said with a wry grin.

"I hear ya."

~ ~ ~

We confronted the Apartments Plus intercom and I buzzed 905. Nothing.

"How are we going to get in?" Ty asked.

I smiled knowingly.

"Don't forget we're with a private eye," Nick joked.

I hit the buzzer for apartment 902 and a female voice answered.

"Hello, yes?" she said softly.

"Jenson Intercoms madam from downstairs," I said sternly. "We've been having problems with the intercom and I need to check yours is working properly, please press your entry button on the count of three ... one, two, three." I ordered with a commanding tone. It buzzed. "Thank you mam yours is working fine. Have a good evening."

"Goodnight," she replied courteously.

We went in to the lobby entered a waiting elevator and I pressed the ninth floor button – it all went like clockwork.

"Clever boy," Nick mumbled inside the elevator.

The next trick would be opening the door of the

apartment, I didn't fancy having to enter from the balcony nine floors up. But when we got to it the door was slightly ajar and I didn't like it, so I pulled my .38.

"Stay here, something's up."

With my gun at the ready I slipped quietly inside leaving Nick and Ty at the door. The place looked the same as it had before – but there was a completely different vibe. I carefully checked all the downstairs rooms – nothing – then gingerly moved up the staircase to the main bedroom door that was closed. I leaned my shoulder against the door gun up ready, turned the door handle with my free hand, and then slowly pushed it open with my shoulder. I wasn't ready for what I found inside. Rosy had been strung up naked from the chains above the bed. She had been disemboweled and her guts were piled in a steaming mess on the bed below in a massive pool of coagulating blood. The look on her face was horrific – she'd obviously been gutted while hanging there alive like a butchered animal. The stench of blood, stomach contents and death was way too much for me. I rushed to the bathroom and threw up. After splashing water on my face, I dried off, holstered my pistol, and then went back downstairs and flopped forlornly on the lounge totally wired with shock.

"Come in fellas!" I shouted dispiritedly.

Nick and Ty entered tentatively and stopped immediately glaring at me in horror. I must have looked like I'd seen a ghost.

"Upstairs," I groaned, "if you can handle it. Don't touch anything."

As it turned out they didn't handle it either. As soon as they both caught the sickly sight of Rosy, hung naked and disemboweled, I could hear them make for the bathroom to throw up their expensive dinners.

After a few minutes both of them staggered back downstairs and sat on the sofa, wide-eyed, jittery and pale faced. I rummaged around, found the bottle of vintage Jack that Rosy and I had cracked earlier, and poured three three-finger slugs to calm our nerves.

"I'd better call the cops," I finally said once the Jack had kicked in.

"No!" Ty erupted. "Not yet, we need to think about this first."

"There's not much to think about Ty, Chiang's missing and now this ..." Nick said.

"It's a murder case now, and unless you want to be an accessory to manslaughter after the fact, I suggest we get my mate DI Malone, here pronto."

"You're right but I just don't want to complicate matters and I don't want the press involved," Ty groaned. "I knew that girl was nothing but trouble."

"Let me look after all that," I said, ignoring his slur and drawing my phone. I called Rick at home.

"Rick, yes, sorry to call you at this time of night but remember the missing person case I told you about, yeah, well there's a development ... a dead body – murdered. No, I rather you handle it yourself. I'm at the crime scene now ... Okay, 905 Shelly Street Apartments Plus. See you soon." I terminated the call and focused on Ty. "He's coming from Coogee, so he won't be long at this time of night. Now look, he'll be on his own – he's an old mate ... I trust him ... he'll be able to keep it under wraps for a while and we can work with him but you'll need to be up front with him Ty. If he gets the drift you're bullshitting he'll throw it to the press, do I make myself clear? I know this guy like a brother, he's one hell of a cop."

"Your word is good enough for me Axis," Nick said looking for confirmation from Ty.

"Okay, I'll have to trust you on this Axis," Ty said unconvincingly.

"Look Ty, whoever did this means business, who will be next, Jazz?" I pressed him.

"What makes you think this is connected with my problems?" Ty said defensively.

"Ah, come on Ty, with Chiang missing and the girl up there, his partner, butchered, someone is sending you pretty heavy message," I growled.

"I think you should listen to him Ty, none of this is looking good for you," Nick warned.

By the time I'd freshened up our drinks Rick buzzed the intercom downstairs.

After introductions I led Rick upstairs to see the body.

"Jesus! Whoever did this sure meant business!" he exclaimed, obviously shocked. "I'd say he slit her open while she was alive and then left her to die in agony. You say you knew her?"

"Yeah, she's Chiang Sun's girlfriend ... I saw her earlier today when I was casing the apartment for clues and get the hair sample."

"Huh, the notorious Chiang Sun ... I checked him out with Bill at the nark squad after you mentioned him in the office. He came up with more markers on him than fleas on a dog – he's got serious form."

"After what happened to Rosy it's looking more and

more like the shark leg is Chiang's," I promoted.

"Granted. I think I need to hear all the facts, let's go back down and talk with your buddies."

On the way out of the bedroom I said, "Can we keep this under wraps mate for the time being? This could be a bloody Chinese gang war and if we expose our involvement whoever did it might well try and knock over more of Ty's family or even Ty himself."

"I'm hearing you," Rick said on our way down the staircase.

We talked it over for an hour, and then once Rick was satisfied with the story he phoned forensics to come lock down the crime scene and turn it over for evidence. Though in reality he didn't expect to find anything – it was a professional hit and it had probably been wiped clean of prints. I worried in silence that when they check Rosy for rape and semen, they'll find my DNA – then I'll have some explaining to do.

~ ~ ~

We took the limo to the Golden Dragon and retired to the private room to discuss our options. It was near 2 a.m. when Jazz burst into the room all in a fluster like a woman possessed.

"I just heard! Why didn't anyone call me?" she all but screamed at us.

"Because it is a police matter, Jazz," I said.

"Come here love, it's good to see you," Nick said, in his oh-so-cavalier manner.

They embraced like old lovers.

"I thought you were only going to be in town a few hours," she said enquiringly and then sat at the table all calm and collected like a totally different person.

"So did I, then this terrible thing happened ... "

"But how?" she queried.

"I found them at Fortune Garden," I said with a wry grin.

"Ty was going to drop me at the airport for the 11.30 to Brisbane. We stopped at Fortune Garden on the way for dinner and a little fun at the tables. As we were leaving Axis got a distress call from Rosy," Nick explained.

"Why did she call you Axis?" Jazz asked indifferently.

"I saw her at the apartment earlier remember. I guess I was the only person she could think of to call when she needed help," I said happy to gloss over the truth.

Before I could say another thing the three of them cranked up in Chinese. It came as a shock to me that Nick spoke it so fluently. I had him figured to speak only Tagalog and English, but then again he did admit to having Chinese blood – I guess the language comes with it.

The Cantonese was getting boring and I was about to nod off when they suddenly realized they were being rude.

"Pardon us speaking Chinese, Axis, we are not intentionally keeping anything from you, just catching up on family stuff," Nick admitted apologetically.

I stood up, "Well, I don't know about you guys but it's been a long day for me, I'm out of here. Good to see you, Nick. Say hi to the girls."

We shook hands.

"I'll give you a ring in a couple of days to see how you're getting on. If you need me for anything please don't hesitate to call," Nick said.

"Thanks, mate," I said appreciatively. "We'll talk

tomorrow, Jazz ... Ty."

I left them to continue chatting in their chosen language and set off to walk home. I was feeling out of sorts, the case was getting to me – I'm more confortable when I'm in control and this one was out of my control. But the cool night air was clearing my head – I picked up the pace – my footsteps echoing off the cavernous city walls – I was alone in Sussex Street and the full moon overhead had my shadow stretched out in front of me like it was another person. I stopped, maybe that's it? I questioned myself – what if it's all smoke and mirrors – shadows in the night? What if Ty really does owe a huge gambling debt? What if he used the deed of the Golden Dragon to secure it and now doesn't want to pay up? I started walking again but this time slower, more decisively. The cool night air had me puffing steam like I was a smoker. What if Chiang was doing a drug deal to pay off the debt that went wrong? Have I been looking at it through the wrong lens? The first law of a sleuth is to establish motive and the second is to determine the most likely suspect – I'd done neither. I resolved to get home and map it out on paper so I could decide what step to take next. A pair of headlights flashed from way down the far end of Sussex Street, which is one-way, by the time I got to my apartment block it had reached me, it was a taxi and he slowed down hoping I was a customer. I pulled my keycard, swiped entry and then passed
through the double glass entrance doors.

CHAPTER
SEVEN

I'd been at it an hour mapping out the players I knew to be involved in the case and listing the different motives, but I was getting nowhere. I needed to speak to someone from Sun Yee On. I relaxed back on the couch. I don't know how many times I've woken up on the sofa in the morning still dressed, and I decided this wasn't going to be an exception. I'd only been asleep a couple of hours when I was jolted awake by the downstairs buzzer. I tried to focus on the time, it was six forty – and then the buzzer sounded again. I got up groaning and answered it.

"Yeah, who is it?"

"It's Jazz. I'm sorry it's so early but ..."

"Come on up if you must," I said tiredly with a modicum of impatience.

I had the coffee on by the time she knocked on the door.

"Come in, it's open," I called from the kitchenette. "I'm just putting on a brew."

When I came out to the living room I found her sitting on the lounge with her head in her hands.

"You all right?" I asked.

She lifted her head and her big brown eyes stared at me. "Just tired," she groaned. "I dropped Nick at the airport and came here because there's so much to discuss ... it couldn't wait."

"It's kept me up as well but the more I thought about it the less I realized I knew," I admitted. "Why don't you just relax and I'll get us that coffee. How do you take it?"

"Just black thanks."

I went back to the kitchen, filled a couple of mugs, dosed up mine with a nip of JD and then juggled them back into the lounge room.

"Here you go," I said handing her a mug. It was then I noticed she had kicked off her shoes and was barefoot. She saw me looking.

"Sorry but you did tell me to relax," she said huskily. "I remember what the sight of bare feet can do to you."

"Is that a threat or a promise?"

She smiled vaguely, "The way you reacted I guess it's a promise."

"I won't hold my breath," I said giving her a vague smile in return.

"We're getting off the track ..." she brought the mug up to her red lips and sipped. "Hmm, nice coffee."

I took the armchair opposite her. "Look, you'd have to say it was the Sun Yee On, who threatened me, killed Rosy Tong and possibly your uncle. I don't think they'd go around killing people so they can take over a property, so there has to be more to it than that."

Warming her hands with the mug of coffee she said, "Go on, you're making sense."

"Nick confirmed Ty hasn't got excessive gambling debts."

"How would Nick know?" she asked.

"You tell me, how close is he to the family?"

"He was close when we were young, he went to school in the UK with Chiang and he'd visit us here during his summer vacation, but that's all."

"How long were you two an item?"

The look on her face tightened, she didn't like the question at all. "I don't see what that's got to do with anything."

"It's got to do with you being truthful, someone from your family has to be."

"Okay, we had sex. He deflowered me, but it was only the once, that one summer when I was sweet seventeen."

"Good."

"But of course you already knew that."

"Yes, but I needed to hear it from you. So would Nick know if Ty was in financial trouble?"

"No. Father is too proud to admit that to someone as wealthy as Nick."

"Okay, then we can dismiss Nick's statement as speculation only."

"Agreed," she said.

"So let's assume that happened, after all you had your suspicions otherwise you wouldn't have sent me to Fortune Garden knowing I wouldn't be able to get into the private club. Testing me huh?"

"Sorry, it won't happen again, you proved your worth. Yes, I've suspected it for some time. He goes there every day for God's sake, sometimes for five or six hours!"

"Do have access to his corporate and personal bank accounts?"

"No way! I'm female, remember."

"Is there an accountant?"

"Yes, Mr. Singe."

"Right," I scribbled his name on a notepad. "Now suppose Chiang was trying to hustle up money to save selling the Golden goose?"

"Very possible, you're thinking illicit deals, like drugs?"

"Yes, and prostitution."

"I wouldn't put anything past Chiang. You name it, he's dabbled."

I stood up and then paced about. "Okay, this is what I need – paperwork on the financial position of the family from the accountant."

"Mr. Singe."

"Yes, can you do that?"

"I can try, but he's not Chinese, he's Indian and will be easier to talk to. What else?"

"I need the name of someone in the Sun See On."

"I don't think I can help you with that ... I can ask around but I'd have to be super discrete," she said with foreboding.

"No, better you don't do that, I'll need to find another way."

She placed her mug on the coffee table, and then got to her feet without hurrying. She crossed to me standing so close her body was almost touching mine.

"There's always a way," she said huskily, looking at me in a misty sort of way.

I felt the breath catch in my throat as she moved even closer until her soft, nubile body was pressing against mine. I could feel the strengthening in my groin, and she must have felt it too, because she lowered one hand and brushed the back of it lightly across my rising cock. "See?" she whispered. "Anything is possible."

She moved back from me, and still with a half smile and that misty look in her eyes unbuttoned her white silk blouse and exposed her breasts. The dark pink nipples of her full breasts stood erect. Then she unfastened the belt of her pants and let them drop. She stepped out of them. She wasn't wearing underwear. I feasted my eyes on her divine legs and her stunning feet. She moved her legs slightly apart so that the hair of her pubis came down to a small black wisp between them. Her slit was open a fraction, just enough for me to make out the tiny pink knob of her clitoris delicately placed between the petals of her portal. Still watching me, she fondled her womanhood releasing even more juice to lubricate the sheath. My prick was fully hard now.

"Do you like Axis?" she hissed, showing herself to me.

"Oh, indeed," I nodded.

"So, let's do it then ..."

It took only seconds for me to tear off my clothes and come to her, my engorged weapon pressing hard against her mound. Taking it in her hand, delicately stroking it with her nimble fingers, she slid to her knees. Bringing her head forward, she brushed her face against my throbbing horn. Her lips parted, then closed around the stem. I pushed my hips forward so that it slid deep into her mouth. She pulled her head away and smiled sleepily at me.

Taking my hand, she led me over to the couch and lay back on it. I brought myself on to her, and within a flash the moist sheath of her pussy was snugly enclosing me. Our bodies began to move in harmony as we drew the passion out of each other, coming faster and faster until we were both powerless to control it. Her fingers dug into my back, and her moans echoed in my ears. Her body arched and twisted beneath me, her legs were drawn up as I pumped vigorously against her. And then, in an overwhelming rush that left us both breathless, it was over. Jazz was most definitely a star!

We fell asleep in an embrace and when we woke a few hours later we made it again. I felt we could keep on doing it all day, sucking her toes and licking her tasty body and then bringing her to ecstasy – then *Someday Soon* broke the rhythm. It was Rick Malone, he needed me urgently at the station.

It was difficult to say goodbye to Jazz, neither of us wanted to risk losing what we'd been enjoying. But it had to be, she walked off home and I caught a cab to Police HQ in Surry Hills.

~ ~ ~

It was a cloudy day, threatening to rain but it didn't matter, I was sitting in the rear of the cab totally on another planet – her scent still on my body, my cock and balls still buzzing with sexual satisfaction.

~ ~ ~

I'd cast off my post sex radiance by the time I sat in front of Rick in his office.

"You look something the cat dragged in," he quipped.

"Been a big night, not much sleep," I countered.

"Look, I got you in because I want to discuss this with you before you go running off and getting yourself into trouble," he said sternly holding up a folder.

"I need a coffee before you lay this on me."

"White and three?"

"Better make it four from memory the coffee here sucks."

"You're right." He picked up the desk phone and pressed a button. "Two coffees please, one white with four sugars and my usual, thanks sergeant."

He handed me the folder and a couple of minutes later one of my less favorite female officers in the world, brought in the coffees. I'd nicknamed her Snap because she growled every time she saw me. Most people wouldn't even think of her as female she was so hard faced and testosterone driven.

"Oh, if it isn't Mr. Little head rules the big head," she snarled upon seeing me.

"Snap, good to see you doing your job, I hope you got the sugar right."

"I should have known it was you ... four bloody sugars!"

"Thanks, Janice," Rick slipped in to put an end to our verbal spat.

She put the coffees on Rick's desk, shot me a look of doom and bailed.

"What is it with you two anyway?" Rick pleaded.

"I don't know, just mutual dislike I guess," I said taking a sip of the coffee. "So, the leg belonged to Chiang Sun, I guess we should expect the rest of him to be hard to find?"

"I reckon so. But it does change the priorities of this case Axis."

"I was going to ask you about that ..."

He'd picked up the phone and said, "Come in now please sergeant."

I was still reading the forensic report when a tall, young, well-built, well-dressed, Chinese guy entered and sat down next to me.

"Axis, this is Grant Lee."

"Hi, Grant," I said taking his hand to shake.

"Grant is with the nark squad under Bill. He spent time undercover with the Sun Yee On, a Triad gang you're familiar with Axis ... I thought he could give you some leads because without getting to them, you'll be just pissing in the wind."

"You read my mind, Rick."

"Why don't you guys go down to the Royal Albert Pub and talk about things over lunch?" He checked his watch. "I'll meet you there in say an hour or so."

"Sounds good." I got up. "Catch you then, Rick," I said.

A quiet guy, Lee didn't strike me as being the kind to go undercover in a gang as barbarous as the Sun Yee On and survive it.

We walked to the pub and went inside. It was only midday so there weren't many patrons and we had our pick of tables. We sat in a corner private enough for what I expected to be talking about.

"Do you want a drink, Grant?"

"Just a fresh orange juice please."

I went to the bar and returned minutes later with his drink and a JD for me.

"I know it's early but it's been a big night. Cheers," I said.

"Rick already filled me in on your case, so I think it's best to tell you a little about what you're up against and how to deal with it."

"I'm all ears my friend."

CHAPTER
EIGHT

An hour later we had devoured a hamburger each, I'd downed two more JD's and the place had filled to the brim with a lunchtime crowd. Along with that I was completely mind blown by what Lee had told me. How he was still walking around in one piece had me totally mystified.

"So even though they're only a small division here they have serious muscle and fingers in every illicit pie you could imagine?" I summed up.

"Yes, plus they're intent on expanding, recruiting. I examined Rosy Tong in the morgue this morning, she was a member – but only a new recruit."

"How can you tell that?"

"The tattoo on her ankle was fresh, you get one immediately after initiation."

"So do you think she was a plant?"

"Absolutely, and an expendable one at that."

"What do you mean?"

"They butchered her because of you."

"What!" I erupted with disbelief.

"Look, they are all about demonstrating their power, that is the Triad lore, a supreme form of stand-over, similar to the Mafia. They knew she was talking to you, they probably even commanded her to do so. Did she have sex with you?"

"Yes."

"Well, there you go, you're a Gweilo man. Very unlikely that she would do that, she wasn't a whore, she comes from a decent family. She was fucking you because she had been told to ... and then her use-by-date had expired. Simple as that."

"Fuck, these people are ruthless."

"Chinese women, especially if they were born here do not risk their reputation by sleeping around, especially with a Gweilo. If you're fucking one, then you can be sure that the higher her status is the less she would be doing it for enjoyment."

The bells were ringing – why did Jazz come from the airport to fuck me? Why had it been so easy for me to fuck Rosy. I felt used.

"Okay, I've learned yet another cultural lesson. Answer me this," I explained the situation with Nick Vargas and how I met him in Manila on the Kitty Lovejoy kidnap case. I also mentioned how he had deflowered Jazz.

"That's not uncommon ... many Chinese girls are deflowered by relatives, especially in the upper class. As much as he is your friend, I think you will find that in this case, blood runs thicker than water. In the Philippines case it was a Western girl, so your friend who had a relationship with the kidnapped victim needed you as an ally."

"Okay, I get the picture. So what do you know about Chiang Sun?"

"Plenty, he had been trying very hard to break into the big time drug trafficking business. He had a massage parlor in Haymarket ... now what was it called, oh yes, *Cum and Go*."

We both laughed at the name.

"From there he ran high-class Asian escorts most to Chinese customers from the casinos. He would source girls from China, fly them here, take their passport, pay them very little, work them to death under the guise of them paying off their debt to him – most of the time they would end up smack freaks and staying on here illegally ... that's what got him into the drug game: the girls need drugs to keep going."

"So the Sun Yee On are the Chinese drug lords here?"

"Yes, you could say that."

"And Chiang needed to deal with them ... but he was 14K."

"Ah, now you've struck a nerve. Old man Sun, the father of Ty and Chiang was a drug lord in China."

"Yes, Nick told me the rumor that he got out of China in 1946 with money he stole from the 14K."

"No not the 14K ... Sun Yee On!"

Suddenly it all made sense. It was a get square, Sun Yee On wanted the old debt repaid.

"So let me get this straight – Ty Sun gambles and runs up debts and uses the Golden Dragon as security – brother Chiang is doing a big dope deal to try and cover the debt, it goes tits up – the debt is called in - Ty has to give them the Golden Dragon but won't – they torture and kill Chiang – but still Ty won't give in ... am I on the right track?"

"I think you're on the money with that hypothesis yes," Lee confirmed.

"So what needs to be done?"

"You must establish if Sun Yee On holds the debt or Fortune Garden, then how to settle it or they will go for Ty Sun's family next and that won't be pretty."

"He's only got a daughter ... Jazz. How would they react if I was to front them?" I asked.

"Who, Sun Yee On?"

"Yes."

"They'd kill you."

"So what can I do?"

"Firstly, let Rick deal with Sun Yee On. Secondly, find out how much the debt is and arrange for Ty Sun to pay it."

"What if he doesn't have the bread?"

"Then he'll need to borrow it. Remember, he would never have mortgaged the Golden Dragon, Chinese don't like borrowing money from banks."

Just then Rick turned up.

"Hey boys. Can I get you both a beer?" he crowed.

"Grant's on orange juice and I'll take a Jack on the rocks."

"I thought it was only Harvey Wallbangers for you Axis?"

"Went off them in the Philippines, too much tropical vegetation."

"Went troppo, huh?" he said with his distinctive Malone chuckle as he headed for the bar.

I left for the office a while later with a contact in the Sun Yee On I had traded with Rick and Grant for a promise to stay out of the investigation into the murders of Chiang and Rosy. There were two sizable things on my plate anyway, one, to tell my clients it was Chiang's leg the shark had thrown up and the other, to find out how much Ty owed and to arrange the debt to be cleared. I would only use the Sun Yee On contact Lee had given me as a last resort, besides the contact was in Hong Kong.

~ ~ ~

Just as I stepped out of the elevator at the office *Someday Soon* cranked up. I answered.

"Stone, who … Nick! Sorry mate I've got a bad signal just here, hang on, " … I moved away from the elevator to the 6th floor landing window outside my office door. "You there, ah, that's better. How you doing mate? They do? Great, send them my love in return. I'm about to tell Ty and Jazz that it was Chiang's leg … yes the DNA was a match. I'm sorry mate. Look, I've just come from a meeting with the cops and a specialist in Chinese affairs … the consensus of opinion is that Ty is in serious financial trouble. I know you said that but maybe Ty is too embarrassed to tell you the truth. Did you notice anything unusual at Fortune Garden when you were there? There you go, if they would only accept your marker and not his … that a sure sign. You do? Yes if you could find out it would be very helpful. Okay, talk to you later. Ciao."

There was a chance Nick's contact at Fortune Garden might be able to tell him the extent of Ty's debt – it was a start. I went into the office and didn't like what I found there – the place had been trashed. Someone had been looking for something and made a hell of a mess trying to find it. I figured I knew who'd done it but had no idea of what they'd been looking for? I rang Lee.

"Grant, this is Stone I just got to my office it's been turned upside down. I don't know. You reckon! They'd do that just to frighten me off? What, don't you think finding

Rosy gutted was enough? I'm glad you understand them mate coz I sure as hell don't. No, don't bother reporting it ... There's nothing for them to find ... I've got nothing. No, they can't knock over my apartment ... it's alarmed. Okay, talk to you later."

The next call was to Jazz to set up a meeting with Ty. I left a message to meet at the Golden Dragon at 5 p.m. in two hours time.

Grant Lee had put the wind up me, so I decided to go home and check the apartment hadn't been trashed as well.

Turned out it was fine. I had time to kill so I decided to clean up the place, it was looking pretty grubby after the torrid session with Jazz earlier in the morning. As I was picking up a glass from under the sofa I came upon an iPod that certainly didn't belong to me. I sat in an armchair and booted it up. Not being up to speed on iPod's, I opened a couple of apps. I wanted to know who it belonged to but didn't know how to find out. I opened settings – that didn't help. I couldn't read any of the social media files they were all in Chinese, which led me to suspect it belonged to Jazz. I opened the photo album and the first photo I saw was a selfie and it was Rosy – the iPod belonged to Rosy. I flicked through the photos, there were over four hundred them. The majority of them were of Chiang with other guys and dolls. *I thought she said Chiang didn't like being photographed ... and she only had the one photo.* To my PI photographic eye most of the photos seemed to be candid or spy shots. Then I found a one taken from the mezzanine of Chiang's apartment looking down. Chiang was in the process of handing over a large sum of cash for what looked like bags of cocaine or crystal meth, and the man handing him the drugs was Sergeant Grant Lee! Suddenly it dawned on me that this was probably what someone wanted badly enough to ransack my office. The important question was: did they want it bad enough to have tortured and murdered Rosy? I scratched my head wondering if the photograph implicated Lee or if he had he been undercover at the time. I double clicked it to find the date: March 17th, 2016, only three months ago. I was under the impression Lee's undercover gig was finished by then – I needed to speak with Malone – this whole thing was beginning to get ugly. I figured it would be wise to hide the iPod, go to the meeting with Jazz and Ty, and dig a little deeper there – wait for Nick to come back to me, then speak with Rick after about Grant Lee once he got home. So I hid the iPod in my secret whippy behind the fridge. A shower and a change of clothes were in order.

All spruced up, I slipped on my trusty .38 and then headed for the rendezvous at the Golden Dragon.

~ ~ ~

There were only a few customers in the restaurant at that hour and a new girl at reception. She had nothing on Rosy, in fact her buckteeth were so bad she'd be able to eat an apple through a tennis racket. She led me to the private room where I found Ty with the same pair of goons guarding him. I stopped inside the door and waited for the goons to leave, eyeballing the one who'd pulled a knife on me last visit. I sat to the side of the table so my back wasn't facing the door – call me paranoid – but at this stage I still had no idea who was kosher.

"Is Jazz on her way?" I asked Ty.

"I've been calling her. Did she respond to your text?"

"No."

"And she hasn't to mine. Should I be getting worried?" he asked.

"Not yet ... let's give her half an hour or so, sometimes women get a kick out of being fashionably late," I said sarcastically.

"In the meantime you obviously have news, there's no need to wait for Jazz," Ty said sternly. "What is it?"

I could tell he'd prepared himself for bad news.

"I'm sorry to tell you that the DNA was a match – the severed leg belonged to your brother." I was being as compassionate as possible. He froze, the color drained from his cheeks and he fumbled his inside coat pocket for something. His shaking hand found the flask and he raised the silver vessel to his mouth and drained it in a few gulps.

Just then the door opened and Jazz entered. We were both relieved to see her. Garbed in a classy brown knee length skirt, a beige satin button up blouse and a salmon cashmere cardigan she looked wonderful. The blouse was unfastened just far enough to elegantly display her stunning, high breasts.

"Sorry to keep you gentlemen," she said sitting down. Immediately upon seeing her father's face her outlook changed. "Is everything all right father?"

"No, Stone heard from homicide that the DNA of the shark leg matches Chiang."

It struck her like a left hook. She instantly burst into tears and then moved quickly to her father and embraced him. They carried on talking in Chinese whispers for the next fifteen minutes while I sat there like a piece of the furniture.

Finally Jazz turned to me and asked, "So are the police now involved?"

"Yes, it's officially a murder investigation. Look, I'm sorry for your loss Jazz but the stakes are getting higher. When I got to my office this afternoon it had been ransacked."

"Why? What would someone be looking for that you would have?" she said crisply.

"I've no idea. The point is we need to get things into perspective. Ty, I need to know the truth … "

He glared at me with fierce eyes and growled, "I don't know what …!"

I interrupted him, "If you don't tell me, the police will find out anyway and all hell will break loose. Do you want that to happen?"

"No way!" Jazz snapped and then scowled at her father. "Tell him, father."

CHAPTER
NINE

It was the weirdest confession I'd ever heard. I'd tipped the right horse all along, Ty was in over his head with gambling debts but there was more to it than that, a lot more. His father Chiang Sun Sr. was vanguard or operations officer for the regional head quarters of the Sun Yee On in Canton, a prestigious job for a Triad. That's where the family got its name, Sun ... Chinese names are pronounced in reverse, so Ty's actual name is Sun Lin Ty. The old man fled China for Australia in 1947 to avoid persecution by Mao Tse Tung's People's Republic Movement. Because he had control of the treasury, Chiang Sr. had helped himself to a grubstake to set he and the wife up in Sydney. After a while, when the Dragon Head – leader of the Sun Yee On – discovered the robbery, he sent an Enforcer, after Chiang Sr. to recover the loot. When the Enforcer confronted Chiang in Sydney, he said he'd taken the money to finance a Sydney branch of Sun Yee On. The Enforcer accepted the excuse returned to China and told the Dragon Head, and so Chiang became Dragon Head of the Sydney chapter of Sun Yee On. There was little activity in Australia to warrant a chapter back then, no room in the Aussie criminal underworld for the Chinese, so the chapter basically fizzled out and by the time Ty and Chiang Jnr. we old enough to take over in the early 1970's, the chapter had virtually ceased to exist.

It wasn't until Lee Tai Lung, Dragon Head of Sun Yee On was assassinated outside the Kowloon Shangri La Hotel in 2009 a change was made in the regime. By then Sun Yee On was in control of both the Hong Kong and the Chinese Canadian Film Industries, perfect vehicles for laundering the proceeds of illegal gambling, drug trafficking, human trafficking, murder and prostitution. It took until 2012 for a new, young Dragon Head of Sun Yee On to be appointed in Hong Kong, and because he'd been educated in Sydney, he decided to step up activities there and try to use the Australian Film industry in the same way as Hong Kong and Canada, to launder their filthy money. When the Hong Kong Organized Crime and Triad Bureau got wind of this they informed their counterpart in the Australian Federal Police, but it was too late for them to stop them, a delegation including the Dragon Head was already in Sydney in discussion with Ty and Chiang Jr.

Now this is where everything started to come undone and led to the current problem. Ty and Chiang rejected the deal from the Hong Kong Dragon Head. Ty wanted no part of the illegal activity. He had built an honest and successful restaurant business with the Golden Dragon and a respectable community profile. The Dragon Head wasn't impressed, he believed the Sun family owed their success and social status to the money Chiang Sr. had stolen from the Sun Yee On reserves in 1947. He issued an ultimatum: repay the debt in cash or kind or there will be serious repercussions ... which is what he is now experiencing.

So in short the demand was: work for us, pay up or lose

the lot.

I asked Ty how much they wanted and he told me ten million dollars.

"What about the gambling debt?" I queried.

"That's just another brick in the wall," Jazz added lyrically.

"Okay, so I get all that but why kill Chiang and Rosy?"

"They murdered Rosy because she had something on them," Ty said irritably.

"That's not all, she was a Tong," Jazz added.

""What's her last name got to do with it?"

"Tongs are a fraternity similar to Triads but more like a Chinese social club, nothing illicit, they are civic-minded," Jazz explained.

"So was Rosy some sort of plant or something?"

"We think so," Ty said stiffly.

I knew she had the Sun Yee On symbol tattooed on her ankle, which would fly in the face of what they were saying but I kept it to myself.

"They killed Chiang to force me to give in to their demands," Ty said spitefully.

I still wasn't satisfied.

"Look, let me put my cards on the table here. I heard from a reliable source that Chiang involved in a big drug deal. Surely, if that went wrong, it could lead to his death ... and if Rosy was spying on the deal, maybe she saw too much."

"I'd check my sources if I were you, Stone!" The last word came out in a full-throated roar.

I rocked back in my chair with my eyes locked on his mulling over his reaction. After a pregnant pause I broke the silence. "You have only four options Ty, pay up, join up, take them on or let the police handle it."

"That seems to be the case," Jazz said morosely.

I stood up and said honestly, "I can't make that decision for you, but one needs to be made and quickly. You know the urgency ... give me a call when you've made it," I growled. "I can't do anything more right now. But there is one more question, was Chiang with the 14K?"

"That would have no bearing on our problem, thank you, Mr. Stone," Ty said dismissively.

Then suddenly as though summoned by magic, the two goons entered the room and stood either side of the door, arms folded like a pair of gargoyles showing the way out. Ty was trying to intimidate me, I wondered why when I was supposed to be working for him. I put it down to him not trusting anybody. My stomach was growling, I was expecting to get fed at the restaurant and dipped, so I walked up to the cinema complex in George Street and picked up an Aussie burger from Hungry Jack's — call me old fashioned but I've just got to have a slice of beetroot in my burger, anything else would be a fraud.

On the way to my office I phoned Nick and filled him in on what I'd learned from Ty. It flipped him out. His contact at Fortune Garden had confirmed Ty was in hock for around two million bucks. We agreed to talk later.

I wasn't looking forward to the chore of cleaning up the mess in my office. I polished off the burger, brewed a coffee, rolled up my sleeves and got stuck into it. Turns out it was good therapy, I had a revelation ... what if Grant Lee was related to Lee Tai Lung, the head of the Sun Yee On assassinated in Hong Kong in 2009. Ty mentioned the

Dragon Head that took over had been educated in Sydney. It was another thing to run past Rick and it reminded me to ring him. With the place spick and span, I sat back in my desk chair and phoned Rick at home. I told him we needed to speak off the record and he got the urgency. He agreed to come to my office – it would only take him twenty minutes. He liked a beer so I ducked up to the corner liquor store and picked up a cold six-pack. By the time I got back he was due. The clock had just ticked over 10 p.m. when he knocked on the door. I let him in and handed him a beer. We sat down, toasted and took a swig of the brew.

"So what was important enough to drag me away from Monday night football?"

"Sorry mate, who was playing?"

"Oh, just the Dragons and the Sharks, don't go for either of them."

"Huh, Dragons and Sharks ... sounds like this bloody case," I chuckled. "I had a confessional with Ty Sun and his daughter Jazz earlier tonight and learned a lot. I'll fill you in on it all but first I need a little off the record info from you."

"Ah, the off the record bit."

"I need to know when Grant Lee finished his undercover mission with Sun Yee On?"

"Off the top of my head I'd say mid last year. Why?"

"No reprisals?"

"No, he only did a report on them, no arrests were made."

"I see," I said suspiciously.

"What are you getting at Axis?"

"Okay, here's the off the record bit ... I found an iPod on

the floor of my apartment that belonged to Rosy Tong, she must have dropped it there the night before she was murdered."

"Stop right there, mate. What was she doing in your apartment?"

"Fucking me."

He slapped his forehead, "Oh shit, Axis! You know what that means don't you?"

"Yes, it complicates things I know, but just bear with me. Everything on her iPod was in Chinese, I couldn't read a thing, but I found a stack of photographs that were dated, and one of them taken only last month showed Chiang Sun handing over a wad of cash for three one kilo satchels of what you'd have to expect to be ice or coke."

"That's the sort of evidence we could do with," Rick said cheerfully.

"Wait there's more ... the guy handing over the ice was Sergeant Grant Lee."

Well didn't that throw the cat amongst the pigeons ... Rick sat there glaring at me like a stunned mullet.

Finally after what felt like ages, he ran his fingers through his hair and said with a sigh, "Okay, naturally I'll need the photograph. This isn't going to be easy Axis, he's one of ours ... but you did the right thing telling me and I appreciate that. I'll meet with Bill first thing in the morning and come up with an MO, but you keep it close to your chest."

"Good-oh," I confirmed.

"That's the trouble these days with ethnicity in the force, it used to be the Italian's that corrupted their own people, now it's the Vietnamese, Chinese, the Pakistani's –

name it, Sydney is a potpourri of ethnic challenges – just like New York. These groups lean on their own in the force and have the means to turn them – I don't know what we can do about it – it's like you've got to look over your shoulder inside the force as much as you do out on the street."

"I don't envy your gig, Rick. There is one other observation. Lee Tai Lung, the Dragon Head of the Sun Yee On was assassinated in Hong Kong in 2009. The replacement Dragon Head was educated in Sydney. You pronounce Chinese names in reverse so Lee is actually the surname ... the question is: could Grant Lee be a relative of Lee Tai Lung? What if he's the bother of the new Hong Kong Dragon Head, they're normally dynasties."

"So are you saying Grant Lee could be a plant by Sun Yee On to ensure the prosperity of their organization here?"

"Yes, and that he might be a more important member than just a plant, he might be the Australian Dragon Head."

"Shit!" Rick exclaimed, and downed the rest of his beer to ease the anguish.

I filled him in on as much of what Ty had told me as I could remember, along with Nick's confirmation of Ty's gambling debt. Rick told me to leave Fortune Garden to him to have vice bust the place.

"Don't let that childish hero-complex get the better of you, if anything breaks, will you, Axis?" Rick pleaded gruffly.

"Don't worry, my friend, I'll work on this with you," I conceded.

It was nearly midnight by the time we'd finished talking, I walked him downstairs to his car and then strolled home.

Just as I entered the apartment *Someday Soon* sounded a message alert. It was Jazz, she wanted to speak urgently and asked me to come to her place. I sent her an okay and she replied immediately with the address: Apartment 1707, The Connaught in Liverpool Street.

It was a trendy address only ten minutes walk from my place.

~ ~ ~

She was waiting at the door for me dressed in a scarlet robe. I followed it down to her bare feet.

"Oh, I should have thought to have worn slippers, come on in Axis," she purred, her sloe eyes watching my face like a hawk.

She flung the door open wide, I stepped inside. I padded across the deep pile carpet, it looked like a page out of *Ladies Home Journal,* the place reeked of luxury – obviously interior decorated by a professional it was more like the nest of a rock star than a highly privileged Chinese chick in her mid twenties. Jazz gestured for me to sit in an armchair opposite her on the three-seat lounge.

CHAPTER
TEN

"Sorry to call you so late Axis but I've only just got back from talking with father at the restaurant. To say he's rattled would be an understatement," Jazz said with a sullen look.

"I'm sorry if I caused that, I might have been insensitive considering the message I was there to deliver."

"No, it wasn't that … we were prepared for the worse with Chiang … it was the realization of the four options that floored him. That's what we've been arguing about since," she said crisply.

I scanned the room, "So um, what's a guy gotta do to get a drink around here?"

"Oh, sorry," she picked up a remote from the coffee table in front of her and pressed a button. A large abstract painting of a naked Chinese girl with lovely breasts on the far wall slid to one side revealing a cavity. A light flickered on inside it and a well stocked bar appeared. "Go help yourself," she said boastfully.

I cruised over to it, "Hmm, this is my kind of bar! What can I get you that you haven't already got?"

"Now that's a leading question, Mr. Stone. You'll find an unopened bottle of Jack Daniels Sinatra there you might like … I'll have one on the rocks with you."

"Sounds like fun but I'd prefer a bed," I quipped.

When I found the bottle the label blew me away, it read: Jack Daniels Sinatra Century Limited Edition Tennessee Whiskey.

"You've got to be kidding this is vintage stuff, it'd be worth at least five hundred bucks!"

"More like a thousand sweetie – I said help yourself didn't I?"

I cracked it, poured three-finger shots into two glasses and added a little ice from a chrome bucket. Walking back to her I savored the aroma rising from the fine drop. She took her glass and we touched them.

"Cheers," I said and then took a sip. "Ah, the nectar of the gods."

"Sit down, Axis. I called you over because father and I came to a decision. I will be calling Nick in a while to ask him to go to Hong Kong to meet with the Dragon Head of Sun Yee On and do a deal."

"Nick? Hong Kong? Why not do it here?"

"Because it's a matter of honor that can only be proposed to the supreme head ... Nick has a good understanding of this, speaks the language, and is family."

"Why doesn't Ty go?"

"We can't risk that. Which brings me to the second part ... "

"There's more?"

"You will accompany Nick."

"Me! In case you haven't noticed, Jazz, I'm a Gweilo!"

"We have noticed, Axis, and that's exactly why you should accompany him. With you there he'll be safe."

"But ... "

"No buts, we're paying you, are we not?" she said flatly.

"Not enough if you're asking me to risk my life being Nick's bodyguard ... that wasn't in the brief."

"Yes, I suppose you're right," she agreed icily.

"I've got doubts about getting paid what's due me! Need I remind you your father is in hock for two mill and change to Fortune Garden ... and as he said himself, ten million to Sun Yee On."

"I will put forty thousand in your account tomorrow. Will that do?" she snapped huskily.

"Plus a first class open date return ticket and a Peninsula Hotel suite, so I can keep an eye on Nick and you've got yourself a deal."

"Done."

I got up. "Mind if I top up?" I continued in an even more casual voice.

"Help yourself," she purred offhandedly.

I went back to the bar, poured myself four fingers and elbowed the ice. The booze was too classy to taint, like W.C Fields so wisely had quoted, *I don't drink water ... you know what fish do in it?* When I turned around she was standing up. She undid the tie around her robe and let it fall open. She was naked underneath.

"Anything else you'd like, Axis?" she whispered.

Her hand unzipped me and caressed my erect cock. Her other hand worked frantically on my clothes until I was naked.

I put my drink down and my hand stimulated her willing slit until she was wet and panting with a longing. She jumped up quickly and wrapped her legs around my body as I guided my rod into her velvety moist cleft. I backed her over to the couch, and as we settled down I felt her orgasm come and mine followed. I gently withdrew and kissed her hard nipples. Her eyes widened sharply.

"Where are you going?"

"To get my drink. Can't let it go to waste."

~ ~ ~

I was in the kitchen of my apartment the next morning brewing a liquid breakfast when *Someday Soon* cranked up. It was Nick.

"Hey, Nick, how goes it?"

"Fine, Axis, so what do you think of their plan?"

"I think it's crazy but who am I to judge?"

"I hear you, I'm not exactly sold on it myself, if it wasn't for you going I wouldn't even consider it," he snorted.

"So you agreed then?" I asked casually.

"Yes."

"When do you want to do it?"

"I was thinking of leaving today ... would you be all right with that?"

"No time like the present mate, sure."

"Jazz said you want to stay at the Peninsula, that'd be my choice as well, so I'll tell her to make the bookings. There's a Cathay flight out of Brisbane this afternoon so I'll get it. She'll get you on the first flight out of Sydney."

"Shouldn't we be flying together?"

"Not necessarily, no one from Sun Yee On will know we're arriving, so there's no danger. That'll come once we make first contact."

"How will we know who to contact?"

"I'll have all that, you just get yourself sorted and I'll see you there. Text me your arrival time so I can have a limo collect you."

"Cool, see you tonight."

I poured myself a cup of Java dosed it up with sugar and milk and sat down to enjoy it when the phone rang again. This time it was Jazz.

"Hey, Jazz," I said easily.

"Hi, lover," she purred.

"Hmm, getting familiar are we?" I jested.

"Why not? I can still feel your presence in my hot pussy," she muttered huskily.

"Wish I could feel that, at the moment Mr. Happy looks like he's on strike."

"Why!" she exclaimed.

"He's not looking forward to going to Hong Kong, he doesn't like staying in doors for too long."

She giggled, "You'll need to be at the airport at midday. You're booked on Cathay flight one hundred that leaves at 1400 hrs. ETA 2155. I've texted that to Nick so he can have you collected from the airport ... and don't worry, Miss Happy will be here for Mr. Happy when he comes back, I promise," she taunted lustfully.

"Okay, he'll see you in a few days. Tell me something, I checked on Wikipedia and it says that well-to-do Chinese ladies only screw Gweilo's for a reason ... what's yours?"

"How about Mr. Happy fills me up ... does that sound reasonable, Mr. Stone?"

"Sure does. See you when I see you."

"Okay, be careful," she added warmly.

She was gone and I was off on another adventure into the unknown this time to Hong Kong with its Triads and Dragon Heads and funny food – good grief! I decided to give Rick Malone a ring to give my itinerary. He didn't think going to Hong Kong was a good idea, but then agreed it was my job to put myself in danger. He told me there had been a resolve to his meeting with Bill, vice would be busting Fortune Garden this week, and Police Internal Affairs were looking into Grant Lee without his knowledge. I gave him the Sun Yee On contact Grant had given me and he reciprocated with the name and contact number of the head of the Organized Crime and Triad Bureau, the OCTB, a division of the Hong Kong Police force.

~ ~ ~

Next I found myself in a big comfy first class seat sipping champagne at 40,000 feet on Cathay Pacific flight one hundred en-route to Hong Kong. Eight hours of pampering and bliss followed – made me feel like Lord Muck. The stewardess even produced a perfect Harvey Wallbanger! I was seriously impressed.

~ ~ ~

I cruised out of the arrival section of Chek Lap Kok airport in no time flat, first class certainly has its advantages at the carousel. After passing immigration and customs I sighted a little guy in a white uniform, his hat bearing the name Peninsula, holding a digital board with a red led light displaying *Mr. A Stone*. High tech I suppose should be expected in this the mecca of revolutionary computerized gadgetry. He led me to a dark green Roll Royce and opened the rear door for me. When I looked inside I found Nick. He handed me an even more perfect Harvey Wallbanger.

"I think you might find this to your taste Mr. Stone." He raised his glass. "Welcome to Hong Kong – the pearl of the orient."

I took the glass and sank into the plush grey kid leather upholstery.

"I thought the pearl of the orient was Manila?" I questioned.

"It's also Sri Lanka and Penang, but none so rightly deserves the crown as Hong Kong."

The half hour trip to Kowloon was spectacular even though it was night with misty drizzling rain. It was especially stunning when we crossed the Tsing Ma Bridge, then through the Tsing Sha tunnel, across a second bridge, Stonecutters, then into Kowloon. When we stepped out of the Roller onto the forecourt of the impressive colonial Peninsula Hotel the humidity hit me like a wet fish. I was instantly reminded of Manila's balmy nights. Though it was twenty-six degrees Celsius the humidity was one hundred percent, certainly enough to cause my armpits to leak like a busted faucet.

There was no check-in needed, Nick had everything under control. He led me to the Peninsula Tower elevator we rode up to the 27th floor. We entered the grand deluxe harbor view suite that put Jazz's plush apartment at The Connaught to shame.

I flopped into a comfy chair and took in the misty but still majestic view of Victoria Harbor and Hong Kong Island.

"This must be costing a penny or two?" I grinned to Nick as a porter delivered my bag.

"Around two and a half grand US a day," he mumbled off handedly, as though it mattered not.

"Holy smoke, we'd better get the job over and done quickly then!"

"Axis, we're here to do a deal worth well in the region of fifteen million dollars, so a few grand in expenses is chicken feed."

"Must feed the chicken that lay the golden eggs," I joked.

We discussed the MO and agreed to be up early to start the day with breakfast.

The alarm woke me at 7 a.m., after shaving, showering and dressing, I headed out to the living area where I found Nick reading the South China Morning Post.

"Good morning mate," I said taking in the remarkable view through the big floor to ceiling windows.

Nick lowered the tabloid, "Howdy, I've ordered coffee and croissants, will that do you?"

I flopped into a chair opposite him, "Stomach's not used to having food this early but we'll handle it."

"I got a text message earlier from Ty with a contact."

"With Sun Yee On?"

"Yes, a guy that knows the way in. As you would imagine it's not an easy organization to get a meeting with, it would be like trying to get an audience with a Mafia Don in New York I expect."

"Yeah, tough ... what's his name?" I queried.

"White Snake."

"What? That sounds a bit suspect."

"Apparently he's a stuntman, one of the best here actually ... we already know the Sun Yee On tie-in with Hong Kong movies, so it makes sense that would be an entry point."

"I guess so."

"I was warned to only ring him after 11 a.m."

"Makes sense. Movie types are generally night-owls," I agreed. "Maybe we should pay the head of the Organized Crime and Triad Bureau a visit first then?"

"The OCTB, I don't know about that ... they're liable to put a tail on us after we blow the whistle and that might cruel our chances of meeting the Dragon Head."

"Yeah, you're probably right. Will my phone work here?"

"Yes, if you've got it on roaming."

"Cool."

CHAPTER
ELEVEN

We finished breakfast then Nick being Filipino, a regular mall-rat, insisted on cruising the Harbor City Mall complex underneath Tsim Sha Tsui. After three hours of walking I'd had my fill of Prada, Ralph Lauren and every other designer label on Earth ... the only thing that kept me occupied was bird-watching – but even that had a low ratio of worthy contenders, nothing like Manila or Sydney. I convinced Nick that I badly needed a coffee, so we returned to the Pen and found a table in the legendary Grande Dame of the Far East lobby. You had to marvel at the majestic vaulted ceilings and ornate cornicing that swept you back in time to when it was built in 1928. Aside from enjoying grandeur unrivaled anywhere else on the planet, I took in the femme fatale parade on display. Seems the lobby was a magnet for the Hong Kong social set to strut their latest designer frocks. It also attracted its fair share of foreign tourists, some interesting others best ignored. I was busy exchanging alluring glances with a blonde Germanic looking piece seated all alone nearby. She had the longest beautifully tanned legs and a bust to die for, platinum blonde hair to her shoulders all garbed up in a cute summer A-line cotton frock that rode up well above her knees. I was just fancying my chances when a nine-foot Viking without the horns turned up and whipped her away.

Nick was on his phone talking with White Snake. He finished just when our coffees arrived.

"Whoa, he's an interesting character," Nick said a little shook up.

"Why's that?"

"He's been in so many Hong Kong action films. You don't really notice stunt men until you've met one. He'll be here in a while, he's just up the road in Mong Kok."

"So do you think he's one of them?" I posed.

"I'd say so, but he won't admit it."

"How did Ty find him?"

"He said he met him with a Hong Kong film director when they ate at Golden Dragon. They were in Sydney shooting an action film a couple of years ago. He told Ty if ever he needed anything done in Hong Kong he'd sort it for him," he said almost eagerly.

"Makes sense Ty would meet plenty of celebrities at the restaurant, it is after all one of the best Chinese feeds in Sydney."

I tasted the coffee and it was extraordinary. "This is the most amazing coffee I've ever tasted."

"I thought you'd be impressed," Nick said with a curt smile. "It's Civet coffee from Indonesia, rare and expensive."

"What makes it so different?"

"It undergoes fermentation inside a Civet … a creature a bit like a possum."

The word *inside* prevented me taking another sip.

"Can you expand on the *inside* bit please?"

"The Civet consumes coffee cherries and then leaves the

beans to be collected later from its faces."

"Its shit?"

"Yes, the Civet emits enzymes during the digestion process that alters the taste of the coffee bean."

"Of course it bloody would," I wiped my mouth with a napkin and put down my cup fighting back nausea.

Nick smiled, "Mate, if I hadn't told you about it you would have continued drinking it believing it was the best coffee you'd ever tasted."

"Mate, if you'd told me you were going to order it I would have said no."

"Ah, come on, drink it up, it's clean and a delicacy worth savoring, its forty US bucks a cup."

"Jesus!" I picked it up and continued sipping. "If you don't think about it and just relish it ..."

"Yes, stunning isn't it?"

Just then Nick's phone rang and as he answered a guy with white hair appeared out of nowhere.

"No need to answer Nick, I was just checking it was you," he growled.

Nick stood and I followed suit. We shook hands with the White Snake, only a small man but with a hell of a presence.

"Sit down, Mark. Can I get you anything?" Nick asked.

He waved his hand "no."

"So do we call you Mark, or White Snake?" I questioned.

"Yeah, being a martial arts master Gweilo meant I was given a Chinese Name. So they gave me two, one that is known only to few and the more general name of White Snake."

"I detect a bit of an accent ..."

"Yeah, born in the UK, came out to Malaysia when I was twelve, lost both parents in an accident. Was adopted by a Chinese family and spoke no English until I was eighteen. I started learning White Crane from a master then changed to Hung Gar under the kung fu master Ho Kam Wai Sifu. I moved to Hong Kong in 1989 when I was twenty-seven to train under master Lau Kar Leung, a famous stunt coordinator, and he got me into movies and bodyguard work ... the rest is history."

He'd obviously told the story plenty of times before because it ran off his tongue like honey. There was no way either of us were expecting a fair haired, hunk of pink skinned Englishman to be our entry point to the largest and most powerful Triad organization in the world.

"Can we talk here Mark?" Nick asked.

"No, it would be better to go elsewhere or up to your room," he suggested.

Nick gave a nod to the waiter and then we headed up to our suite.

~ ~ ~

Mark was wearing a black sleeveless vest, black jeans and red Converse runners. His muscly arms told the tale of years in the gym. The elevator was so crowded I had to stand behind him. He was only five nine so I was looking down on him and could see the edges of colorful tattoo that must cover his entire back. I could also see masses of deep scars on his bare shoulders and lower neck. By the time we stopped at the 27th floor we were the last in the elevator. Being nosey I was anxious to ask him about the scars.

We entered the room.

"I've been in this room a couple of times now, " he said. "Actors like to stay here."

We sat down facing the big windows.

"What a view," I said.

"Yep, its a pretty city," he said admiringly.

"Can I get you a drink?" I asked.

"Never touch the stuff, tell me what you need? I owe Ty a favor," Mark said with a steely smile.

I'd seen his type before, friendly but cool, calm but with shark eyes – just like Ringo Raye my gangster nemesis on the last case in the Philippines, only Mark was gifted cobalt blue eyes instead of tawny. Certainly not a guy to mess with, unlike Ringo I reckoned this guy could cut you down in a flash and not necessarily with a weapon, just with his fists.

"We need to make contact with the Dragon Head of Sun Yee On," Nick said tightly.

"Excuse me Axis but I need to say something to Nick that I cannot express in English," he said carefully.

I nodded okay and he spoke in fluent Cantonese and Nick replied. They kept it relatively brief.

Not wanting to exclude me Nick told me, "He asked me if Ty was in trouble and I explained the circumstances."

"It's okay, I understand. So can you help?" I asked.

"It will take a couple of days but I'll do my best, no guarantees. If you have a contact in the OCTB I hope you haven't told him you are here," he warned.

"No, I do have a contact but I would only use it if all else fails," I admitted, a little sheepishly.

"You're a sensible private eye, Axis. I have worked with a couple from the States. Do you know Danny Green?"

"From San Francisco? I've certainly heard of him but

never had the pleasure, "I confirmed.

"If you don't mind me asking, how did you get the scars on your back?"

He stopped, waited a couple of beats, and then eyeballed me. "I got chopped up and left to bleed to death in alleyway by a gang of Triads with meat cleavers. Why - Because they didn't like me - when - twelve years ago. By the time I dragged myself up the alley to a main street and finally got to hospital, I had one fluid ounce of blood left in my entire body – I should've been dead." The naked savagery in his voice sent a chill up and down my spine.

"Satisfied?" He said and I don't think he blinked once through the entire spiel. "I'll meet you at the Four Fingers Club in Mong Kok at midnight. A card game in the back room, you won't be asked to play. There will be powerful Triads at the table ... they will be watching to determine if you are copacetic. Do I make myself clear? You will be tested." He eyeballed us one at a time - the chill made it down to the soles of my feet. I just nodded with my mouth open. I'd met plenty of tough guys before but when it comes to heavy with a capital H, this bloke took the cake.

Nick walked him to the door and let him out. When he came back he flopped into a chair and let out a long sigh.

"Phew, that guy was heavy duty."

"Better get used to it mate, I think things are going to get even heavier," I said gravely.

By the look on Nick's face I don't think he was too thrilled about the idea.

~ ~ ~

We burnt the rest of the day sightseeing on the Island and then back to Kowloon side for dinner at one of Nick's favorite restaurants, Jimmy's Kitchen. He promised there would be no nasty surprises on the menu and he was right, it was probably the best rib eye steak I'd ever eaten. The maître d knew Nick and so we were treated like royalty. We polished off a couple of bottles of fine red wine and by the time we rolled out of there we had wobbly knees.

Kowloon was alive with people at that time of night and it took us a while to catch a cab. Nick had looked up the address of the Four Fingers Club on the directory in our hotel room, so he knew it was near the famous Temple Street night markets. We finally caught a cab and within twenty minutes were let out at Temple Street.

Part of the street was closed off at night for the market, which was in the process of closing down as it was near midnight. We walked down Saigon Street, to the corner of Battery Street and looked for the club. Lucky I was with Nick because the sign to club was in Chinese; it was the only neon in that section of the otherwise dark and sinister backstreet.

"It feels creepy here," Nick said.

After some of the stuff we'd been through together in the Philippines, I had learned that if he said that then he smelt danger. I felt it as well. I'd walked the cobblestones of many ominous red light district dark alleyways in my time, and this one certainly had the hallmarks of the underworld.

"You're not Robinson Crusoe there, mate. You could cut the air," I grated.

Nick opened the door to the club and I followed him inside. It was then I sorely missed my trusty .38 companion. A rogue's gallery inhabited the place, every one of the twenty or so patrons seated at the ten or so tables in the dimly lit room immediately turned their dials to us. Skeins of smoke drifted through room and a guy standing under a single spot on a tiny stage was killing "My Way" – I can't stand bad karaoke. Why people pay money to sit around and put up with mostly untalented, half inebriated, over fifty-year-old executive businessmen singing out of tune has me completely beat. I'd rather watch a tumble dryer, at least it stays in tune.

We ignored the lack of applause and made our way down the six or so stairs into the basement-type club. Nick nodded at two big goons standing either side of a door at the rear of the room. A bar extended the length of the side wall with a few people seated at it on stools. Seemed out of balance, mostly guys, only two or three chicks in the entire room. I followed Nick to the back of the room. He spoke to the goons in Chinese, all I recognized was *White Snake* – they let us through the door. A moldy smelly corridor was leading us to the toilets, when we came upon another door in a recess - this one had an old-fashioned speakeasy peephole window and a knocker. Nick knocked. The viewer opened and a tawny eye gazed at us from the other side of the door.

"Fuck, this is a trip into the past. I feel like Philip Marlowe," I mumbled with my best Bogart impression.

Nick chuckled. The latch clunked, the door creaked opened and we were ushered inside by a stunning looking Chinese babe dressed in a red cheongsam that clung to her shapely body like cling wrap. Things were certainly looking up.

CHAPTER
TWELVE

The gambling room left the rest of the club for dead. This room had class, albeit Chinese taste with loads of red and gold in the décor. Center-room was a large round table at which were seated a dozen men playing cards. Into the light that hung over their heads rolled a haze of smoke rising from cigars – seems that health regulations didn't apply here. Mark was one of the players who looked our way, stood and then approached us.

"Glad you could make it guys ... I won't make any introductions, that's not done. Do you want to sit in and play or sit at the bar?" He half whispered gesturing at the bar that ran along the sidewall. "Or you're welcome to sit at a table over there and have Suzie serve you."

He was referring to several small table settings away from the card game.

"We won't play, we'll just take a table and enjoy Suzie's service," I said easily.

He went back to the game while we pulled up a couple of chairs at a table. Suzie floated over to us as if on a cloud, and with a sultry smile handed out menus. It was all Chinese to me but Nick got a handle on it.

"You hungry or thirsty?" he asked.

My eyes were on Suzie. "I'll just take a JD on ice."

A blink of her eyes told me my order had registered with her.

"Tea for me please," Nick added, gentlemanly.

I watched her lovely little round posterior waddle off on her way to fill our orders and couldn't help wonder if I could make a play on her.

I leaned over to Nick and in a hushed voice said, "Is this like a Makati girlie bar, can I bar fine her you reckon?"

"No, I don't think so, you'd have to go to the Gweilo bars in Wan Chai if you want to chase pussy."

If you listened real hard you could hear a Chinese pipa playing at low level on the audio system. Only muffled sounds came from the poker players, so it was a little like being in a library. Suzie returned with my bourbon and a pot of green tea for Nick.

While she was pouring the tea I asked, "Can I buy you a drink Suzie?"

"No thank you sir," she said behind a stony frown. Before I could ask anything else she fled like she feared I was going to latch my teeth into her. Nick laughed.

"Axis, you kill me, there's never a dull moment around you."

"My motto is *you only get what you ask for*."

"That makes a lot of sense ... I like that, mind if I use it?" he said happily.

"Yeah, what is it with you Asian's can't you invent anything of your own?"

"Not when we can copy it," he chuckled.

~ ~ ~

We'd been sitting there three hours, I'd downed four JD's and Nick was on his second pot of tea when Mark ambled over to us.

"The game is just about finished, come again same time tomorrow night, you might find it more productive."

Nick stood. I was feeling miffed but followed his lead.

"Thank you Mark," Nick said graciously.

Suzie arrived with the bill and Nick paid in cash. She then walked us to the door ... on the way I asked her, "How about lunch with me at the Peninsula today?" Her eyes flashed at me like a warning. "Meet me at 1 p.m. in the lobby, I'll be waiting there for you," I muttered, secretly.

Without acknowledging my invitation she opened the door for us to leave.

There were no cabs nearby so we had a fifteen-minute walk to Jordan Road, before we could hail one.

We reached our hotel room about an hour later. With little to discuss due to nothing happening, we hit the hay.

The next morning started with *Someday Soon* for me. It was Jazz eager to hear what we'd achieved. There wasn't much to tell her but she was impressed with us meeting White Snake and that we'd been invited to the Four Fingers – seems she understood what went on more than I did, saying that in a typical Chinese way the Sun Yee On had invited us just to see what we looked like and how we reacted at being ignored. She agreed the next visit would result in us making contact.

Nick locked in lunch at the Royal Hong Kong Yacht Club with a business associate. I got the address and told him I'd meet him there later convinced that Suzie would turn up for our lunchtime rendezvous.

~ ~ ~

It was one fifteen and Suzie hadn't shown. I was about

to call it a day when I noticed an exotic stunner dressed in a beige trench coat wearing dark sun glasses, glide into the lobby – I knew it was her. I confronted her.

"Suzie good to see you, just for a moment there I thought you were going to stand me up," I said warmly.

"Take me to your room," she said like a spy in a James Bond movie.

I bought into the espionage vibe and did as she requested.

We entered the room and she immediately peeled off her coat, black wraparound sunglasses and sat in a lounge chair.

"Why all the secret agent stuff?" I asked, in a mild voice sitting opposite her.

She crossed her legs they were bare, slender and beautifully shaped.

"I work for very dangerous people," she said with a heavily accented voice.

"So what, you don't have any freedom?"

"Let's just say it is restricted. What do I call you?" she said softly.

"Axis."

"What do you do, Axis?"

"I'm a private detective."

"Hmm, how exciting."

"It has its ups and downs."

I studied her deliberately; the delicate beauty of the oval face with its high cheekbones, the slender grace of her body, the small, twin-peaked perfection of her breasts, the softly rounded curve of her hips. It caused a little ache in my groin.

"What do you want from me, Axis?" she said cheekily with pouted red lips.

"I want so much to have you right now it hurts," I said.

"Then?"

"You want me. I want you. What could be more simple than that?"

As she spoke she pulled the sweater up over her head and threw it onto the chair. Then she unzipped the slacks, pulled them down over her thighs and stepped out of them. That left her in a skimpy black bra and panties.

She looked at me expectantly. "Do you like what you see so far, Axis?"

"Yes, I like," I croaked. Her skin was like ivory.

She reached behind her, and unfastened her bra, tossed it to one side. Her small cute breasts fell free. The ache in my groin became something more positive.

"So let's get to know each other then," she said quietly, watching me with a misty look in her almond shaped eyes as she peeled away her briefs. Then with an air of triumph she stood in front of me, inviting me to feast my eyes.

It was a lot to take in at a glance. Her body was delicate perfection, even more tantalizing and desirable than Jazz's or Rosy's. Her small pink nipples were erect, and through the wispy black hair that covered her delta, the pink pear drop of her clit.

It was two hours of unadulterated lust. She was an expert, and knew just what to do with her hands and mouth to extract a pleasure so powerful that I felt I was about to explode into thousands of tiny pieces. Once, just once, while we were recovering our strength for the next engagement, and just as her fluttering fingers worked to revitalize my half-flagging cock, I wondered idly if we could keep doing this forever. Ah, but sadly all good things must come to an end and she disappeared into the concrete jungle of Hong Kong at 3 p.m. leaving behind only the fragrance of our union.

~ ~ ~

I walked into the Royal Hong Kong Yacht Club and fronted the reception. The girl behind the desk was most alluring I figured by the look in her eyes she fancied me. As she wandered off to get Nick, I thought how lucky I was that Asian women found me sexually attractive – it meant for a whole new outlook as to my sexual preferences in future. One thing for sure, so far I certainly hadn't been let down by their sexual dexterity.

Nick appeared down the corridor and waved me inside. I followed him into the bar where his friend was waiting.

"Ian, I'd like you to meet Axis Stone, the chap I was telling you about," Nick said nautically.

Ian was a big burly yachtsman with a Canadian accent. We shook hands and sat down.

"Nick was telling me about your little South China sea adventure," Ian chuckled.

"I guess he also told you it developed an allergy to all thing maritime and it wasn't *little*," I countered.

We all chuckled.

"What will it be, sportsman?" Ian asked.

"A Harvey Wallbanger minus vegetation," I said with a smirk.

Ian ordered the drink and when it turned up I was suitably impressed.

"A little more civilized than the Manila Yacht club you

think, Axis?" Nick said smugly referring to the drink.

"You bet ya!" I said. "Cheers!"

Turned out Ian was a lawyer as well as being the head navigator for the RHKYC. He been on every South China Sea yacht race since 1986, and had a collection of more seafaring tales than Herman Melville. But it was in his capacity as a lawyer I found what he had to say about Sun Yee On and the 14K, most interesting.

"There has been a war on the streets of Hong Kong between the rival gangs since the handover in 1995," he explained.

"Haven't they always been adversaries?" Nick questioned.

"Yes, but not here, this was mainly the territory of the 14K and that all changed after the handover. Basically they're fighting for control of the underworld. Hong Kong has always been a place of law and order – the cops the law and 14K the order – there was an understanding of sorts – the Poms knew how to handle that with experience in Northern Ireland and India, but once they departed so too did the alliance. Sun Yee On moved in big time and quickly took over the lucrative Hong Kong film industry."

"So the fight continues then, which is stronger of the two?" I asked.

"That depends, 14K have the largest numbers but Sun Yee On are the more influential," Ian explained.

"Which has infiltrated the cops?" Nick asked Ian.

"Now a question like that could get you into real trouble, but I'd have to say that would be Sun Yee On."

"So have you heard of an expansion to other countries?" I pressed.

"Well you only have to follow the Hong Kong film industry to answer that. Canada, Hollywood and now as I understand it they're making moves in Australia."

"Yeah, well, that's how we see it as well," I said.

"Look, you have to be very careful sticking your noses into Triad business here, you just never know who you're talking to and these people are ruthless. Only last year an extremely wealthy friend of mine was found in Hong Kong harbor with a bullet hole in the back of his skull. Seems he had been bonking a Triad's girl. Even with all his money he couldn't buy them off – first he knew of the threat was when he was crossing Nathan Road at the lights in the middle of a workday. A guy came up behind him and stabbed a long thin razor sharp stiletto blade through his pants into his asshole, slashed it from side to side lacerating it big time, and then moved off like a phantom without my friend seeing him. He couldn't sit down for weeks, couldn't shit without excruciating pain – but he kept right on bonking his concubine and before long they dragged him out of Hong Kong harbor."

The thought of Suzie being the girlfriend of a Triad suddenly set off a gong in my mind.

"Yes, they use the same ploy in Kuala Lumpur. I remember reading how the assassin carries a long thin blade concealed inside a folded newspaper," Nick explained.

"Yes, the job is normally part of the initiation of a young inductee," Ian added.

"He just walks up behind you and with a speedy stab, swish, swish, swish ... you're done," Nick said with a macabre grin.

I winced, imagining putting up with that much agony.

CHAPTER
THIRTEEN

Nick wanted to take the Star Ferry back across from Hong Kong to Tsim Sha Tsui but when I reminded him *again* to my aversion of all things maritime, he agreed to take the MTR.

We boarded the train at Tiu Keng Leng Station. Being rush hour it was packed to the rafters. Squeezed in the carriage like a sardine, I figured every dude carrying a newspaper was suspect. I maneuvered myself against a pole so that no one could get at my ass with a stiletto.

By the time we got out at Tsim Sha Tsui Station I was sweating up a storm. It felt good to shake off the anxiety and breath in the polluted air when we emerged onto Nathan Road.

As we walked the congested pavement towards the Peninsula Hotel I admitted to Nick, "Suzie turned up."

"You're kidding me ... you're amazing mate. So what happened?"

"We went up to the room and fucked like teenagers for two hours."

"I'd never have believed she'd be the type to go off like that," Nick said wide-eyed and disbelieving.

"I must admit it stirred the old worry juices hearing Ian talking about retribution for bonking a Triad's girl."

"Why? Wait a minute, is she...?"

"Well she told me she is sort of imprisoned by someone, so I assumed ... you know, with her being a stunner and all that it would be someone from the club ... someone high up ..." I said dully.

"You're thinking she might well be a high ranking gangster's girl?" he rasped.

"Um, yes, I suppose I am."

"Didn't you think to ask her?"

"Well I didn't want to put a negative spin on things ... you know ..."

"Axis, your little head overruling your big head is very likely to get you into deep shit."

We walked into the lobby of the Pen.

"Nar, I don't think so. How would he find out ... anyhow, we'll be out of here in a couple of days ... nothing will come of it ... it was just a good bonk."

We entered the elevator. The moment after I pushed the button and the doors closed, the elevator gave a cultured sigh and came to rest on our floor.

"I wouldn't think someone like that would take too well to a Gweilo doing the business if he found out," Nick said sternly.

"Don't be a racist," I snapped jokingly.

"I mean it Axis, the guy Ian told us about was a Gweilo."

Once again a shiver ran up my spine causing the hairs on the back of my neck to stand on end.

~ ~ ~

We both had a little afternoon siesta and woke at 9 p.m. Nick ordered us room service and the customary exceptional service had the food on a table in front of us within twenty minutes. I picked up a French fry and chewing it gazed out the window at the Hong Kong skyline. The night was clear and Hong Kong was lit up like fairyland.

"Mate, I don't feel comfortable about going to that club unarmed. What about you?" I grated.

"I didn't get it off with Suzie so I'm not sure I have the same degree of concern as you," Nick admitted.

"It's not that as much as I have this gut feeling ... you know what I'm saying, when I get it I've got to listen."

"Danger, you sense danger?"

"I feel anxious ... so yeah, I guess it's probably danger."

"Well, there's not much we can do about it mate, this is not Manila or Sydney, we can't get you a gun ... we'll just have to rely on Mark. Do you feel okay about him?"

I thought about it for a second or two then replied truthfully, "I don't know, something feels uncomfortable ... I can't quite put my finger on it."

"You know I once dropped an expensive gold cufflink from my shirt when I was walking back to my room here at the Peninsula. When I discovered it missing I rang the reception and ten minutes later a bellhop turned up with it."

"Did he find it?" I asked.

"No, they just replayed the video of me walking up the corridor to my room and saw it drop."

It suddenly dawned on me what he was suggesting.

"You're saying they would have video of Suzie visiting me. Damn, of course they would, I should have known that!"

"That's what I'm saying Axis, when it comes to your little head taking control you lose your rationale. I think that's what you're feeling mate ... subconsciously you know damn well that you've let down your guard. Somebody could be studying that video right now."

"I guess you're right."

"Was it worth it?"

"She was spectacular!"

"That's not what I asked."

~ ~ ~

A few hours later we were getting out of a taxi at Temple Street. There seemed to be fewer people around than the night before maybe because the weather had taken a turn and it was raining lightly.

When we entered the club there was a notable difference as well, it was empty – not a soul only a barman and the two goons standing beside the door at the end of the room. This time they let us pass without question and we approached the red peephole door. Same routine, it opened but not to whom I expected, it wasn't Suzie ... in fact it's wasn't even female. He led us inside. There were only eight at the table playing cards and no sign of Mark. We sat at the same table as before and ordered the same drinks from the waiter. It was going to be a long night without Suzie to flirt with and no Mark. The atmosphere made me feel uneasy.

"Something's wrong here," I whispered to Nick.

"Yes, it feels claustrophobic."

The waiter returned with the drinks. Nick asked him in Chinese if Mark was expected. When he left I asked what he'd said.

"He said he knows nothing."

About an hour later Nick's phone rang. When he answered his face turned pale. He hung up quickly and said, "That was Mark, he told me to get out of here like right now!"

Nick signaled the waiter and then paid the bill. We got up and calmly made for the door. None of the poker players paid any attention to us at all. We made it all the way through the club outside onto the street with our hearts in our throats. We had no idea what we were afraid of but Nick still had on his frantic face as we gazed through the drizzle up the dark street. We knew that any chance of getting a cab was at least fifteen minutes walk away. Then I saw someone move in the darkness along the street a little. Then another … I whispered to Nick, "There are guys up ahead hiding and waiting for us."

"What should we do?" he said nervously.

"Either go back inside or make a run for it," I growled.

"Mark said to get out, so I guess we better hit the toe!"

"Okay, let's run in the opposite direction to them and then cut up to Temple Street."

"Got it."

"Ready?"

"As ready as I'll ever be," he said anxiously.

"Okay, let's go!"

We took off like we were coming out the blocks for the two hundred meters at the Olympics. As we rounded the corner into Saigon Street, I was in the lead and ran straight into two guys obviously waiting for me. Both were armed with nunchucks. It was like a Bruce Lee film, with me on the wrong side. I skidded to a halt and shaped up, they were broad but shorter. Nick stopped beside me and copied my pose. There were footsteps from behind. I sighted three rubbish bins and quickly grabbed two lids and handed one to Nick.

"Use it as a shield," I croaked.

I charged one of them and felt the blows of the nunchucks on the metal dustbin lid. I gripped the handle and pushed towards him with all my force driving him into the wall. I could see his legs below my shield so I kicked at his shins ... that stopped him striking with the nunchucks and gave me the chance to whack him with the lid. I collected him right on the chin and it cut his face open. I followed it with a flurry of punches and he went down. The battle behind me was loud. The guy had bashed Nick's shield so hard he had him on his knees. Three more ninjas in black hoodies arrived. I saw the chrome glint in the light of a nearby street lamp – it was a meat cleaver. I launched my shield at the guy bashing Nick collecting him on the back of the head – it split open and blood sprayed on my face. It gave Nick the chance to get to his feet, he was shaky, we were surrounded, outnumbered ... it didn't look good. They closed on us – then suddenly out of nowhere a flash of white and our assailants began going down one at a time. It was White Snake, he was on his own and making minced meat of them. Talk about Bruce Lee, White Snake was really something to watch, he carved them up big time. The guy with the meat cleaver went for him and Mark kicked it out of his hand and then pulverized his face with a barrage of deadly kicks. The guy hit the deck like a sack of potatoes to lay motionless in a puddle of blood. I was enjoying the spectacle when suddenly the lights went out.

~ ~ ~

When I opened my eyes I had no idea where I was except that I was flat on my back looking up at a ceiling light. I sat bolt upright and it hurt so much I fell back.

"He's awake." I heard but couldn't recognize the voice. "Where am I?" I growled, and that hurt as well.

A face that didn't ring a bell came into view – a western face – a woman.

"Who are you?" I mumbled.

"I'm Kerry, you're in my apartment."

I knew the accent.

"You're an Aussie."

"Yes, so are you," she said.

I looked at my body. My shirt was off and my ribs bandaged – I was in my underpants. I felt cold.

"Brrr, it's cold."

Kerry covered me with a blanket.

"Sorry love, but I only just finished bandaging you up when you came around. You took a battering."

"Is Nick?"

"Yes, your friend is in the other room, he's in better shape than you but he's got some bruises and a split eyebrow. He's resting."

"And Mark?"

"Mark!" she called out.

Next he was looking down at me with a cheeky smile.

"You fought well my friend, I could get you a gig as a stunty," he mumbled with a evil chuckle.

"No thanks I couldn't afford the insurance," I struggled to say. "Have I got broken ribs or something?"

"No, just bruised, one of them put the slipper into you big time while you were on the deck, after he'd king hit you."

I felt my left ear it was ringing and hurt like hell.

"Yeah, that's where he hit you – mind you he blindsided you – never saw it coming. Kerry stitched your ear up so it'll be fine, just a war wound," he said.

"Bloody hell you did a job on them," I rasped.

"I'm only sorry I didn't get there earlier."

"Who the fuck were they?"

"I was just telling Nick in there, they were 14K. We got word there was going to be an invasion, you guys just happened to walk out of the club right into it. But listen, a few bumps and bruises but now the Dragon Head owes you one."

"Yeah, why's that?"

"He was playing poker. He came to meet you and was definitely the target of the 14K attack. You guys stopped the attack, so yeah, he owes you."

Seems we had broken through and made contact. Not exactly how we would have preferred it but nevertheless we'd succeeded, and the way it happened, probably put us in good stead.

"Where are we?"

"This is my friend Kerry's apartment in Mong Kok, not far from the Four Fingers. Lucky she was home and could tend to your wounds, she's a nurse."

"At least she knew what she was doing," I said with a sigh.

"Yeah, she treats animals every day with wounds like yours," he grinned.

"Animals?" I hollered.

"Yeah, she's a veterinary nurse."

"Fuck me!" I laughed ... and it hurt like hell.

CHAPTER

FOURTEEN

In the morning a car took us to the Peninsula. We entered our room like the walking wounded. Nick ordered coffee from room service and we sat down to talk with Mark.

"Just exactly who is to blame for the attack Mark?" Nick growled.

It wasn't often Nick showed his anger, but in this case he was livid.

"It is difficult because the 14K have no Dragon Head. You should have heard of them Axis, they're very active in Sydney."

"I'm only just learning about Triad's in Sydney, Mark," I grunted, still aching.

"The most likely suspect is Won Kuok-Lim or as he is better known Broken Teeth-Lim. In 1999 he declared himself Dragon Head of 14K, but it is rumored someone within the 14K blew the whistle on him to the police to get him put away because factions didn't want a Dragon Head. He was released from prison in 2014 after serving fifteen years for murder and has been making moves to take over the film industry since. I reckon he's solely responsible for the increased attacks on Sun Yee On, like last night."

"So does he have the support of the 14K?" Nick asked.

"We think some but you must understand, the 14K are

the enemy of Sun Yee On, and are extremely violent, it is difficult to find out much about them but it is speculated that Broken Teeth was behind the assassination of Lee Tai Lung, Dragon Head of Sun Yee On, outside the Kowloon Shangri La in 2004. That's really all I can say fellas. I have to go now. You will be contacted."

"Thanks for everything Mark," I said taking his hand.

Nick walked him to the door. When he came back he said, "That was pretty surreal last night, I still don't know what happened. Last thing I remember is you using a rubbish bin lid to crunch a guy belting me with nunchucks ... next minute I woke up this morning with Kerry trying to feed me orange juice through a straw."

"We were lucky to get out of it alive mate. If it hadn't been for Mark, we would've been minced meat."

"I don't know about you but I feel like minced meat," he said, feeling his cut and swollen eyebrow.

"Those stitches look okay not a bad job for a veterinary nurse." The look on his face was priceless.

"A what?" he demanded.

"She treats animals, not much difference I suppose ... look she stitched my ear up ... did an okay job didn't she?"

Nick took a look, "Yeah, I suppose so."

~ ~ ~

We rested all day and by nightfall after a bottle of JD to reduce the pain, we were both feeling a lot better. Nick had spoken to Ty and told him what had happened, he repeated his warning to leave the 14K alone and to focus on Sun Yee On. When Nick questioned his reasoning, he simply stated that 14K have a strong presence in Sydney and Manila, and it wouldn't be worth making enemies of them. Nick suggested the beating we took meant we were never going to be friends. Ty reckoned we might have got off lightly.

Just after 8 p.m. we got a call from the front desk to say there were three gentlemen to see us. Feeling nervous as to whom it might be Nick asked for one of them to be put on the phone. He spoke to him in Cantonese then hung up.

"I told them to come up, he said they are friends of White Snake."

"Quick, ring Mark and ask if this is normal," I said hurriedly.

Nick dialed Mark. "Message bank, what do you want to do?"

"You show them in," I said jumping up and slipping behind the door.

There was a knock. I winked at Nick, he opened it and showed them in. I let them pass then stuck my finger in the middle of the last guy's back and growled, "Hold it right there or I'll let you have it ... put your hands up."

He froze and slowly raised his hands. The other two stopped, went to turn and face me.

"Keep looking straight ahead!" I growled. "Nick, frisk them," I ordered, sharply.

Nick patted them down one at a time.

"They're clean," Nick said sternly.

"Okay, you can lower your hands, the three of you sit down," I ordered, keeping my hand in my pocket foxing I had a gun. "You," I picked the more regal looking of the three. "Who are you and what do you want?"

"My name is Lee Kok Lung mister Stone," he said calmly and soft spoken. "I am Dragon Head of Sun Yee On. This is Red Pole, Fatty Tung and with his hands raised,

White Paper Fan, Soy Ling Chu. We are here because White Snake informed us you wanted to meet us to discuss the debts of Sun Ty."

Nick spoke up diplomatically, "I'm Nick Vargas."

"I know of you Mr. Vargas ..." he said then carried on in Cantonese.

"I think it would be best to speak English for Mr. Stone's benefit," Nick suggested.

The threat had passed so I gestured for us all to sit down.

"You can lower your hands Soy," I growled.

"Your finger is not like a .38, Mr. Stone," Soy said with an icy smirk.

"Last night I wished it was a .38, it would have saved us a beating."

I didn't recognize any of them from the poker table but then again, sometimes it's difficult to tell Asian's apart.

Lee was around forty-five I guessed, with thick black hair shot with gray, and an air of obvious authority. His eyes were deep-set, and black like piss-holes in the snow, and his lips were thin set in a straight line. Soy and Tung on the other hand were a bit younger and less well groomed. Tung was tubby with a moon face while Soy was skinny and rat-faced.

"We are very grateful for your brave stand, Mr. Stone and Mr. Vargas," Fatty said with a strong accent.

This guy had a distrustful glint in his eye that I didn't take to at all.

"And we are thankful for the courage of White Snake," Nick countered.

"He has been a valued servant for many years," Lee

admitted.

"Let's cut to the chase, Mr. Lee," I said challengingly.

Soy answered on his behalf. "Mr. Lee is prepared to waive the debt for a half governing share in the Golden Dragon restaurant. Ty Sun would still head up the company, but without the deciding vote. In addition he will work with an appointed manger from Sun Yee On."

I looked at Nick and he raised his eyebrows. I nodded for him to continue.

"What happens if Ty Sun and his family reject the offer?" Nick asked.

"Then he must pay up," Soy snapped.

"And how much is that, Mr. Soy?"

"Two million in gambling debts and of course repayment for the money taken in 1947 ..."

Nick cut him off," Mr. Sun can attest for the gambling debt but there is no record of any debt from 1947. I'm afraid it dwells only in the world of myth."

"All legend is based on fact, Mr. Vargas, so if Mr. Sun would like to settle the debts we will establish in the total an estimated figure for the 1947 debt."

"And if he doesn't agree to any of the terms, Mr. Lee?" I said eyeballing him.

"Then things could become unpleasant for Mr. Sun and his family," Soy answered.

"My question wasn't directed at you, Soy," I said keeping my eyes locked on Lee.

"He speaks for me, Mr. Stone," Lee said in an expressionless tone.

"So this isn't really a business discussion, its extortion," I growled, stink-eyeing Soy.

"Call it what you wish, Stone, that's how we do business," Fatty Tung snarled at me.

There was a pause for the smoldering tempers to cool.

"What are your plans in Sydney?" I asked calmly.

"The 14K have infiltrated the film industry and drug trafficking there – they've forged an alliance with 5T, a Vietnamese organization. Together they now plan to take over the Chinese gambling business controlled by Sun Yee On. We will stop them by whatever means," Soy said zealously.

"What has owning a restaurant got to do with that?" I growled back at him.

"Together with Fortune Garden, the Golden Dragon will add to our influence with the Chinese business community," Lee suggested diplomatically.

"We will need to discuss your proposition with Mr. Sun," Nick said.

"I would be best to meet on my junk *Tai Lung* at Aberdeen at 7 p.m. for dinner and hopefully a resolution," Lee said, standing ready to leave.

"I don't like boats," I complained.

"The Tai Lung is moored, Mr. Stone. It won't be going anywhere."

We shook hands with each of them and they left. I knocked up a couple of drinks, and then Nick and I sat down to discuss the deal.

"I got bad vibes from Soy Ling. I don't trust him at all. What's a bloody White Paper Fan anyway?"

"I think he's an administrator, like an accountant, and Fatty Tung is a Red Pole, an enforcer," Nick explained

"So Fatty is the muscle and Soy the brains?"

"Yes, I guess you could say that."

"How do you think Ty will take the offer?" I asked.

"By the sound of it they're not giving him much choice, but he'd sooner lose control of the company than lose face or his life."

"I think you better phone him, he might need some time to mull it over," I maintained.

Nick drew his smartphone and dialed. Just then the house phone rang. I answered – it was Suzie – she was in the lobby.

I left Nick on the phone to Ty and went down to meet her.

~ ~ ~

I found her sitting alone at a table. "Hey, Suzie," I said sitting down opposite her. She peeled off her sunglasses and looked at me with a horrified stare.

"What happened to your face, Axis?"

"I was on the wrong side of a fight last night. That reminds me, why weren't you at the club?"

She looked very sexy dressed in a just-above-the-knee length navy blue skirt and a brown jacket over a beige blouse. Her legs were bare and very inviting. She crossed them when she noticed me staring.

"I was told not to come to the club last night because there was to be trouble," she said flatly.

"Yeah, well, the trouble found me. Who told you?"

She looked down embarrassed, "My boyfriend ... he arranged the attack, I'm sure. I heard him talking on his phone. It was staged to frighten both of you."

"Staged? What! Who is this guy? You've got to tell me, love."

"His name is Soy Ling Chu," she said disconsolately.

"Soy! The White Paper Fan!"

"You know him?" she said surprised.

"He just left us no more than twenty minutes ago. You're lucky he didn't see you!"

She bit her bottom lip and looked about worriedly.

"Axis, I come here to warn you not go to the meeting on junk. If things don't go their way they will kill you. I overheard Soy telling Fatty Tung."

"I don't believe this. Where? How?" I questioned.

"I was in car this morning when he talking to Fatty."

As she was becoming more upset her English was getting worse. She stood up, looking very nervous.

"I must leave, if Soy find me gone ... he beat me."

"You risked you life to warn me, thank you," I stood and kissed her gently on the lips. I wiped away a tear trickling down her pale cheek.

"Please be safe, Axis. I want see you again," she said softly.

She turned on her heel and rushed off quietly sobbing. I wasted no time in racing back up to the room to tell Nick.

~ ~ ~

He was reading the newspaper when I stormed into the room.

"It was a set up!" I snarled.

He put the paper down. "Sit down. What do you mean?"

"That was Suzie. You won't believe this, her boyfriend is Soy, the White Paper Fan ... he warned her yesterday not to go to work at the Four Fingers because there would be trouble. She said the fight was staged to frighten us."

"What? You've got to be kidding," Nick said astounded.

"Yes, but what's more she overheard Soy telling Fatty Tung in the car this morning that if things go wrong on the junk tonight they're going to kill us."

"Jesus Christ!" Nick bellowed. "That also means Mark's in it with them and can't be trusted."

"What did Ty say?"

"He needs time to think like you assumed – his first reaction was no. He'll call back later with a decision. Now I see the value of your liaison with Suzie, I'm sorry I doubted you."

"I don't think we've got much choice with this mate ... we're going to need the cops."

CHAPTER
FIFTEEN

I rang the Organized Crime and Triad Bureau at the Hong Kong police and asked for my contact: Detective Inspector Shun Zhong. It took a couple of minutes but eventually I was transferred to his cell phone. When he answered I told him who I was and that I'd been given his name by DI Malone and why. I explained what had happened last night and outlined the meeting we'd just had and the fear for our safety after what Suzie had said. He told me to stay put - he was only half an hour away.

I answered the door to DI Zhong. He didn't look like a cop, nothing like I'd expected. Dressed in smart casual attire, he looked a lot like a younger version of Chow Yun-Fat of Crouching Tiger Hidden Dragon fame. I introduced myself and then took him over to meet Nick. We sat down to talk.

"Can I get you anything?" I asked.

"No, I'm fine thank you."

His English was excellent, aged about forty five it was easy to see that he'd been through tough times ... scars marked both eyebrows and there was a coldness about him that only comes from having seen and done terrible things.

"Can you tell us anything about these guys Lee Kok Lung, Fatty Tung and Soy Ling Chu," Nick asked.

"They are the big Triad – Lee Kok Lung is Dragon Head of Sun Yee On. He is the oldest son of Lee Tai Lung who as Dragon Head was assassinated in 2004. Lee Kok took power as Dragon Head in 2006, after he graduated from a Sydney University. His younger brother by ten years Lee Kit Wo, is believed to be currently studying in Sydney. As for Fatty Tung he has a record as long as your arm, as does his sidekick Soy Ling Chu. I've personally been trying to bring those two down for the last ten years."

"Could the younger brother be Dragon Head of the Sydney chapter of Sun Yee On?" I questioned.

"Could be but we don't have much intelligence on that chapter as you would understand."

"I ask because if things go wrong here, there will be reprisals in Sydney and we don't want to put the Sun family at risk," I explained.

"You should have the family under protection until this is over," he said unyieldingly.

"You're right Shun, is that what I call you?" I asked.

"No, call me Zhong."

"What's your call on tonight?" Nick queried.

"You can trust the warning Suzie gave you because she is the girlfriend of Soy. Though we must ask why she has warned you."

"I had sex with her," I admitted.

"Okay, that explains it but makes it even more problematic. You are lucky that she has taken a shine to you Axis, she might have saved your life."

"I appreciate that Zhong," I said shaking my head at the close call.

"What about Mark ... White Snake?" Nick asked.

"He's one of their enforcers, stay away from him, he plays both sides of the fence for them," he said seriously. "Tonight you will have to go in armed and with back up. I know the junk; we've had it under surveillance for some time. I can't go in with you, we can't get a warrant – it would be too dangerous for anyone to go with you anyway. Irrespective of what Ty Sun decides, you know there will be serious consequences – it is only a matter of whether you want to confront them here or in Sydney."

"Are you saying tell them what they want to hear then deal with it in Sydney?" I posed.

"Yes. The alternative is to bring it to a head tonight, have a shoot out and still have to deal with it in Sydney."

"With all your experience with the Triads what would you do Zhong?" Nick asked.

"If it was the 14K, you would have to fight right here and again in Australia, but with it being Sun Yee On, I'd agree to their terms then I'd get to the younger brother and make it clear that if anything happens to any member of the Sun family then he will go down."

"Then what ... pay the money and give them control of the restaurant?" Nick questioned.

"I think gaining the upper hand is the answer and you won't be able to do that here, but you could do it in Sydney. Ty Sun would be no fool, he must be a clever businessman, he will know exactly what to do once he has attained the power position in negotiations," Zhong said.

"Whoa, that's Chinese logic for you ..." I said, battling to make sense of it.

"Very sensible," Nick said, and then added a few paragraphs in Cantonese.

By the expression on his face Zhong was surprised Nick was so fluent. I let them chat while I charged up a glass with bourbon.

"Axis," Nick said, "I'm going to phone Ty now for his decision. I will then explain the plan Zhong has outlined. Okay by you?"

I sat back down and took a sip of my drink. "Yep, that's best."

Nick dialed Ty and then rattled on in Cantonese. After a few minutes he handed the phone to Zhong, and then he rattled on for another few minutes.

"Zhong's explaining the idea," Nick told me.

"What's his decision?"

"Ironically he'd drawn the same conclusion. There's nothing to gain here except accepting the deal. The rest has to be fought out in Sydney."

"I'd better give Rick Malone a call and put a heavy watch on Jazz and Ty."

"Good thinking," Nick agreed.

While Zhong was still talking to Ty, I phoned Rick and filled him in. He reminded me I'd not sent him the incriminating photo of Grant Lee and Chiang. I apologized and promised to get it to him upon my return. I asked if he could do me one last favor … to check police records and find out if Grant Lee is his full name. He agreed, stating it wouldn't take him long and that he would text me the result. In closing he asked me to bring him back a present from Hong Kong and to watch my ass. I hung up at the same time Zhong did.

"I've arranged with Sydney Homicide for surveillance on Ty Sun and his daughter Jazz," I announced.

"Good, that's one part of the puzzle complete," Nick said. "How was Ty?"

"He's fine, he agreed totally with the MO. He knows more than I expected about the ways of Sun Yee On and agrees he'd rather have them as an enemy than the 14K, but at the same time knows that having either of them as enemies is not desired position," Zhong told us.

"Well unfortunately you make your bed and you've gotta to lie in it?" I said.

"Very good Axis, with quotes like that we'll make an Asian out of you yet," Zhong joked.

"Don't worry, from the last case he had in Manila, he's practically and honorary Filipino!" Nick wisecracked.

"If we live through tonight I'll expect the same from here," I added.

Zhong reached inside his coat and produced a holstered .38 and handed it to me.

"Here, you will need this. Its not police issue and unregistered – I didn't give it to you, but I want it back, preferably unfired. Nick, are you okay with being unarmed?"

"You bet, happy to leave that to Axis."

I saw Zhong out.

We had an MO, now we had to pull it off without stopping a bullet.

A few minutes later *Someday Soon* sounded an incoming text.

"It's from Rick, I asked him Grant Lee's full name on police records, its Lee Kit Wo, isn't that the name of the younger brother to Lee Kok Lung? I questioned.

"It sure is."

"So now the suspicion that the Dragon Head of the Sydney chapter of Sun Yee On is Grant Lee, a detective in the vice squad, is almost validated."

I immediately sent Rick a text to alert him of our suspicion.

"A bird in the hand is worth two in the bush," I told Nick.

"I agree, it's an advantage knowing Grant Lee is the Dragon Head's brother, and you're doing the right thing by keeping that a secret there."

"That's exactly what I'm telling Rick," I said, typing my reply to his text.

~ ~ ~

Early afternoon had me needing rest and repair for the big event tonight. Nick bailed out to trawl the malls for a present for Kitty, so I kicked back to watch ESPN. Suddenly it struck me that if it goes tits-up tonight and Zhong and his men have to make a stand, Soy will know it was Suzie that blew the whistle on him. Going on what she'd said about him, it would be like signing her death warrant. With no means to contact her I racked my brain on how to save her, then noticed Zhong's calling card on the coffee table. I immediately dialed his cellphone and laid the problem on him. He said there was nothing we could do for her ... we just had to hope nothing goes wrong and then no one will get hurt. I knew he was right, I guess I'd panicked.

~ ~ ~

At first glance Aberdeen gave me the impression it was like 21st century meets the 19th Century, with thirty floor skyscrapers hugging the foreshore looking down at a view of stacks and stack of junks anchored in the bay. I could see why they were called junks: most of them were like something someone had thrown out.

Soon as I stepped out of the taxi at the wharf the stench hit me, whoa was it ripe. Seems more than junks had been dumped in the water. A faint lapping sound got louder as we walked along the wharf towards what we figured to be the Tai Lung moored at the end.

"I'm still not thrilled about going on that bloody thing," I grumbled to Nick.

"You won't get seasick, it's moored ... unless of course a massive storm hits," he looked up, "and that's not likely, it's not even rainy season."

"Thanks mate that makes me feel so much better," I said facetiously.

Someday Soon played two bars then stopped. It was a pre-arranged signal from Zhong that he and his men in position for us to go ahead and board the Tai Lung.

As foul as the air was, the harbor was lit up like fairyland. But I wasn't in the mood for taking in the sights because tonight was all about self-preservation. A huge six floor barge painted in rich colors and decorated all over with lights was floating out in the middle of the bay with a big green neon sign on the upper deck saying Jumbo.

"What's Jumbo floating out there?" I asked Nick.

"A famous floating restaurant ... you catch a water ferry out to it. When you order seafood on board you select what you want from a huge variety of fish, lobsters, crabs and abalone that are alive in tanks."

"Wait," I stopped him and held up my phone to pose for a selfie with the Jumbo in the background. "One more." I positioned the Tai Lung behind us. "Cool, I hope we get to look back on them in years to come."

"I hear you. So do I," Nick agreed.

I'm sure we both had knots in our guts. It's not easy to walk into a set-up knowing you might not walk out of it.

We were close to the Junk. I looked down at a smaller boat moored at the side of the wharf and caught sight of Zhong on it – that was a relief. I pouted my lips to Nick in the direction of Zhong Filipino style, and he seemed encouraged.

The rotund form of Fatty Tung appeared on the deck of Tai Lung and he waved us aboard. We followed him down a companionway into the main cabin where we found Lee and Soy seated at a round table, similar to the poker table at the Four Fingers. As a matter of fact the interior of the junk was decked out as lavishly as the gaming room at the Four Fingers, and surprisingly spacious. Lee rose to his feet but not Soy.

"Gentlemen, good to see you, please be seated at my table," he said happily, as he filled a small cup in front of each of us with tea from a pot. I took a sip; it was Jasmine.

"Tasty," I said eyeballing Soy who was busy avoiding eye contact. I watched Fatty sit and felt reasonably comfortable with only the five of us present.

CHAPTER
SIXTEEN

"You have a nice junk Mr. Lee, how old is she?" Nick asked.

"She belonged to my father and carries his name," he said calmly. "He built her in 1950."

"How long were you in Sydney?" I queried.

For a split-second I had the rare experience of looking into a man's eyes and seeing a true reflection of what went on in his mind. The ice-cold ferocity of his hate hit me with almost a physical force: then, the next split-second, it had vanished and his eyes were back to normal. Just like the eyes of a shark.

"I compliment you on doing your homework Mr. Stone. I completed a four year degree in business strategy at the University of New South Wales," he said.

"Almost an Aussie then are we?" I said sarcastically.

"I'd like to think so, I have many friends in Sydney."

"And a brother of course," I probed a little deeper.

Soy cut me off rudely. "Let's get on with the business at hand."

There was a pause while I drilled Lee with a cold hard stare, to let him know I was pissed off at Soy's indignant interruption.

"You'll have to pardon Soy, Mr. Stone, he has another

appointment soon in Mong Kok."

Nick coughed to get attention and spoke up to cool things down. "I have spoken with Ty Sun and he authorized me to accept your terms of offer."

"Not good enough Mr. Vargas," Soy snapped at him.

"It that not what we agreed?" Nick responded indignantly.

"I think Soy is saying we don't trust you, nothing personal, but we need to hear from the horses mouth," Fatty Tung growled testily but with a wry smile.

I could tell by his expression Nick was offended, he moved sharply to reach into his jacket for his cellphone. Fatty and Soy, flinched thinking he might pull a gun. I noted by their hand movements they were both packing. They relaxed when Nick showed them his phone.

"You can see by the ID that I'm dialing Ty Sun," he said displaying the phone and then putting it up to his ear. "Hello Ty, this is Nick ..." he clicked on speaker and then carried on in Cantonese. After a few sentences he handed the phone over to Lee, who continued the conversation in Chinese. All the while I was eyeballing Soy ... he made my skin crawl.

Lee finished the call and handed Nick back his phone. They spoke in Cantonese, and then eventually reverted to English.

"I am satisfied with the arrangements," Lee confirmed to me.

"Too easy," I said and stood up from the table.

"Sit down Mr. Stone ... we haven't finished yet," Soy snarled at me.

I glared back angered by his surly attitude.

"What's your problem Soy, you act like you missed out on getting an after dinner mint?" I snarled.

He stood slowly and fronted me. "I don't like you Stone."

"Well you know what, I don't like you more. Now, are we done here or what?" I glared past Soy at Lee.

Soy and I had squared off like a pair of prizefighters at a weigh-in press conference.

"You're just a waste of fuckin' space mate." I said snarled at him.

He shook his head at me contemptuously.

Nick rushed to the rescue, "Is there something more you wish to discuss Mr. Lee?" he asked in a mild voice.

"I don't think so Mr. Vargas," Lee said easily. "I think you should leave now," he announced before I had time to open my mouth.

Soy sank back into his chair and a hoarse whisper came from him in Chinese – it had a frightening undercurrent of tension hovering around breaking point ... I guess he was pissed.

I waited a couple of beats for added impact eyeballing the crap out of Soy. Then when Nick shook hands with Lee and Fatty, I followed suit but passed on Soy out of distaste.

"We won't be staying for dinner then? Thanks for the tea," I said cynically.

I let Nick lead the way out.

We got up on the deck and Nick climbed onto the wharf. Suddenly I heard my name shouted loud and urgent. "Stone, look out!"

I looked sharply up to see Zhong, he'd called out from the edge of the wharf, with arms extended, pistol gripped in both hands aimed at me. Bang! He fired and I heard a loud clump hit the deck behind me. I swiveled around sharply to see Soy on the deck with a bullet hole in his chest taking his last gasp of air while blood frothed from his snarling mouth. Next to his hand on the floorboards lay the .38, he was obviously about to shoot me with when Zhong spied him. A loud thunderous roar like a Rhino charging preceded Fatty as he emerged onto the deck with a gun in hand and a face as red as beetroot.

I whipped out my .38 and shoved his face. "Fuckin' forget it Fatso!" I ordered, and he dropped his gun like it was a hot potato. Suddenly cops appeared from everywhere. Three of them leapt onto the Junk, two drove him down onto the deck hard while the other cuffed his hands behind his back.

I climbed up onto the wharf and immediately shook Zhong's hand. "Thank you my friend, guess I owe you dinner."

"The pleasure was all mine Axis, believe me ... any excuse to take out that asshole."

"I won't be needing this any longer thanks," I said handing over the piece.

"What are you going to do about Lee, he's still on board?" Nick asked Zhong.

"He knows we can't touch him without a search warrant, he'll just sit tight making calls to arrange bail for Fatty until we've gone."

"Can't you charge Fatty?" Nick asked.

"No ... what with ... carrying an illegal firearm? He'd get off that in a flash. No, the only time we ever win is when we catch one of them in the act of a committing a crime. With your help tonight we did that and got one of them. Can I run you back to the Pen?" Zhong asked casually.

"Yeah, would appreciate that?" I said.

"What, don't you want to have dinner on the Jumbo?" Nick quizzed me with a smug look on his dial.

"You'll not get me on another boat mate," I jeered. "Every time I go near one of the bloody things I nearly get killed."

~ ~ ~

We said goodbye to Zhong inside the car out front of the Peninsula.

"I'll need a statement from both of you. Can you draft it tonight then fax it to me?" Zhong asked.

"No worries mate, cheers," I said shaking his hand.

"We'll probably fly out to Sydney tomorrow morning, so until next time," Nick said reaching over from the back seat and taking Zhong's hand.

"You've got my contact details, keep me updated on how you get on."

We got out of the car and went inside the hotel.

~ ~ ~

I flopped into an armchair in the room.

"Well," I said with a sigh, "we live to fight another day."

Nick sat opposite with his head in his hands. "I'm going have to start getting paid for these gigs."

"Surely you don't need the money?"

"I'll need a lot more to pay my insurance if this keeps up," he chuckled.

"Maybe we should be partners ... Stone and Vargas – private detective agency ... sounds cool."

"I think I'll make old bones if I don't take you up on that

offer mate."

The house phone rang, Nick was closest and so answered it.

"Hello, oh, hi, yes one moment." He covered the receiver with his hand and whispered, "It's Suzie."

I nodded to take it and he handed me the phone.

"Hi, yes, I'm all right but not Soy. He tried to shoot me and got himself killed." The phone fell silent while she processed the news. I glanced at Nick.

He whispered, "She'll need to get out of town. Tell her we'll arrange for her to stay at my house in Manila. There's a Cathay flight to Manila tomorrow morning at nine and one to Sydney at the same time."

He was right ... it was the safest course of action. No doubt Fatty would come after her once he got out of the clink. I told her and she was relieved.

"I'll get you an air ticket don't worry. Do you want to stay here tonight?" I asked, she couldn't, there was too much to take care of – it was going to be a drastic life change for her. I wasn't really up for her tonight anyway, aching all over.

What's her full name?" Nick asked.

"What's your full name, babe ... for the ticket? Suzie Wong, I should have seen that one coming," I joked. "Okay, so meet me in the Peninsula lobby at 7 a.m. Yes, then we can go right to the airport together. Okay? Don't be late, bring your passport. Bye." I hung up not convinced she was safe.

Nick looked up from studying his iPhone, "I've booked CX901 to Manila for Suzie Wong and we're booked on CX139."

"Good, what's our ETA?" I asked.

"Um, 8 p.m. subject to winds of course."

"Thanks for helping out with her Nick," I said graciously.

"Hey, what are friends for … if it wasn't for her we might have been killed tonight."

I struggled up and then staggered over to the bar to pour myself a drink.

"I'll just text driver Dom to pick her up at the airport … whatever you're having I'll have one as well."

That was a turn up for the books, Nick rarely indulged. I poured two, neat, two finger bourbons and added a few cubes.

"I feel like I've been through the mincer," I said carrying the drinks back walking like an octogenarian. "You better give Kitty a call and tell her you're okay."

"Good thinking, I'll do that. Why don't you ring Jazz, to let her know we survived," he said taking a glass from me.

"I'll do that right after I guzzle this lovely drink. Cheers to cheating death yet again Mr. Vargas." I toasted.

We clinked glasses.

"Ahh, the best pain relief I know," I said satisfied.

~ ~ ~

I couldn't sleep, even after half a dozen JD's, I was just too worried about Suzie. Around 2 a.m. I dropped a sleeping pill, next minute I felt someone shaking my shoulder and I sat up in bed with a jolt. It was Nick and it was 6 a.m. time to get up.

Glaring at my dial in the mirror trying to shave, I found it difficult to raise my left arm due to my bruised ribs. As for my face, the black and blue bruising had come out – that along with the torn and stitched up left ear made me look like I'd just been three rounds with Mike Tyson.

Nick's the perfect bloke to travel with, he's so together and neat it stinks. While I was in the bathroom going through my morning ablutions, he ordered breakfast and fixed the bill, so all I had to do was pack my few things and I was ready to rock. We threw down a croissant and a cup of coffee and then headed down to the lobby.

~ ~ ~

There wasn't much activity at 7 a.m. a couple of those types you always see in hotels wearing a headband and lycra off for a jog in the pollution ... and then a few like us with bags under their eyes and at their feet checking out.

Nick went out to the forecourt to supervise the loading of the limo while I sat in a lobby chair on the lookout for Suzie.

Every now and then I checked the clock on the wall behind reception, at 7.15 I was beginning to get nervous. When it got to 7.25 I sighted Nick making his way toward me – I figured he wouldn't be able to hold the limo much longer.

"We've got to go Axis," Nick said sorrowfully.

"I hear you." Feeling glum I picked myself up, grabbed my port and walked slowly toward the main doors where the limo waiting on the other side.

CHAPTER
SEVENTEEN

I just reached the big double glass front doors of the Peninsula when I heard a small voice at back of me call my name. I turned so sharply it hurt. It was Suzie, struggling with two big bags hustling her way from the eastern entrance. I thanked heaven even though I'm agnostic.

Nick was relieved to see us make our way to the Roller. It was another sultry day – misty rain – I was glad to be leaving, even though I never really got a taste of the fantastic city. We climbed into the Roller.

"Nick, you know Suzie?" I said.

"Hi, Nick. Axis told me 'bout you," she said coyly. "I remember you from Four Fingers."

"I only told her the good stuff, Nick," I said with a chuckle.

"So we are going to Manila?" she asked.

"Um no, you're going to Manila," I said with a frown.

She looked down like she was about to cry. "But I don't know anybody there and I have no money to find a ..."

Nick chimed in, "It's okay, Suzie. We owe you plenty for saying our lives ... you're most welcome to stay at my house for as long as you like. My driver Dom will collect you from the airport."

"Where you going?" she asked, as a single tear descended her pale cheek.

"To Sydney ... we have business there," I told her.

"Axis lives there, Suzie, but I live in Manila. I will be in Australia for a couple of months then back to Manila," Nick explained carefully.

She had a sad, lost puppy dog look on her face, so Nick expanded on what he had been saying in Cantonese and that seemed to brighten her up.

It was a somber trip to the airport, the weather outside the limo gloomy, the feeling inside the limo gloomy. I held Suzie's hand on my knee and wished we had time to make love once more. I looked at her bare legs protruding from her red dress and at her red shoes – she reminded me of Dorothy in the Wizard of Oz. She crossed her legs and the back of one shoe slipped off her heel. The sight of her pretty foot tuned me on, and I delicately moved her hand off my lap so she didn't feel Mr. Happy rising to the occasion. I looked out the window to take my mind off it, but saw her reflection – her ruby red lips, her black shoulder length hair with a curl that gave it life and a lift. I imagined her going down on me – I closed my eyes – it was worse: I saw her naked in my minds eye – Nick spoke up just in time.

"Next time you come to Hong Kong, Axis, make it springtime. It's lovely then. We can play golf ... I've got an actor friend with a helicopter, we could have had some fun dropping in on some of the islands to play."

"Hitting the islands would be fun but the golf with all things maritime – is a no-no I'm afraid. Last time I played golf, it was at Bonnie Doon in Sydney. I played so lousy I threw my clubs into a lake and walked off the course – never played again. I'm left handed and play right handed – get that."

"Pros say that's the best combination, it means your strongest arm pulls through the shot," he said, imitating the motion with his hands.

"That'd be fine if I could hit the ball in the right direction ... I'd need a GPS in the ball to find it. That last game ... I think by the fourth hole I'd lost six balls."

We laughed and my mind was at last above my belt.

It was a sad scene at the airport. It felt like I'd known Suzie for years. I hate goodbyes and this was an academy award winning performance, she clung to me sobbing like a child. I promised to call her regularly and that I would come and see her soon. By the time we boarded our flight I was emotionally exhausted.

~ ~ ~

I slept like a baby most of the way to Sydney and missed out on indulging in the wonderful Cathay Pacific first class treatment, though the stewardess gently covered me in a blanket once I'd curled up in the big comfy seat to sleep. I did however get to treat myself to a perfect Harvey Wallbanger and a plate of scrumptious hors-d'oeuvres before we touched down in good ole Sydney town.

~ ~ ~

There was no reason for Nick to stay in Sydney. He'd booked a domestic flight to Brisbane.

"You okay to handle this without your sidekick?" he questioned.

"Yes, Tonto, I can deal with it."

We hugged as good mates do and watching him head for the domestic terminal bus I bellowed after him, "Hi-yo

Silver!"

That turned a lot of heads and a young boy about eight cruised over to me, put his hands on his hips militantly and complained, "Hey you're not the Lone Ranger, anyhow It's Hi-*ho* Silver, not Hi-*yo* Silver! ... and where's your mask?"

"Go check your Wikipedia, son ... and, I couldn't wear the mask through customs they would have thought I was a terrorist," I told him doing my best Lone Ranger impression.

He went running back to his mother screaming, "Terrorist! Mum, that man's a terrorist!"

Fearing I might get arrested I quickly hopped a cab for the city.

~ ~ ~

It felt good to be back in my flat. I immediately went to my secret whippy and retrieved Rosy's iPod. I flopped onto the lounge to work out how to get the photo of Grant Lee and Chiang off the device to send to Rick. I gave up and decided to ask someone more tech savvy like Jazz. I was just about to phone her when the intercom buzzed. I answered – it was Jazz – so I buzzed her up. I put the iPod back and quickly tried to clean up the flat. My ribs killed me every time I bent over, so I wasn't thinking of bonking Jazz, but then again I thought, a few painkillers I might get the urge.

A knock at the door sent me to open it. I flung it open ready to give her a big hug and copped punch in the face. The force reeled me backwards and I hit the floor hard and banged my head so it nearly knocked me out. Blinking my eyes trying to stay conscious, I peered up through the flying stars to see two burly guys standing over me with stockings covering their faces. They looked surreal but the reality was

146

one of them had a gun pointed at my face and the other was holding a baseball bat.

"Get up," the guy with the gun ordered.

I wasn't about to argue and struggled to my feet holding my throbbing jaw. Another guy pushed Jazz ahead of him through the door. The three of them were Chinese their looks accentuated by the tight stocking covering their faces. I'm sure one of them was the big guy that whacked me in the office a week ago.

The guy holding Jazz savagely pushed her onto the lounge then barked at her in Chinese, I guess to stay put while he viciously gagged her. Her face looked pale, panicked, her normally neat and tidy image all roughed up. But to her credit she wasn't whimpering, to the contrary, she had a look in her eye that given half the chance she'd rip her attacker's head off. We exchanged a glance and her eyes soften for me.

Whack! A pistol smacked me in the temple and sent my head reeling.

"Where is the photo?" The guy who'd whacked me demanded through clenched teeth with a heavily accented voice.

"What fucking photo!" I snapped back at him as a warm rivulet of blood trickled down my cheek from a cut eyebrow.

"Okay, have it your way Gweilo! Hold her!" he ordered aggressively, and the two guys took Jazz by the arms.

"Lift her!" he growled.

They rough-handled her to her feet. She struggled against their grip but there was no point, they were too strong for her.

The dude with the gun kept it on me while he backed

over to Jazz. When he reached her, he ripped open her blouse. She wasn't wearing a bra so her full breasts fell out for all to see.

"Cut one of her tits off!" he growled.

One of the guys holding her pulled a switchblade from his pocket, flicked it open, and held it under her right breast ready to slice.

"Wait!" I shouted hurriedly. "Do it and you'll get nothing from me! I'll give you what you want. Just let her go! "

The guy with gun nodded at Fatso. He took the knife away and pushed Jazz back onto the lounge. She struggled to cover herself.

"Get it!" the gunman ordered.

I held my hands up, "Okay, okay, take it easy … no one's trying to resist you." I struggled to my feet, "It's in the bedroom," I said and with raised hands and led him there. The .38 was in the bedside drawer. I thought about it but decided against going for it for Jazz's sake. I carefully retrieved the iPod from where I put it and handed it over.

"There, I guess this is what you're after. The photo is on it."

"Show me!" he said jabbing me in the ribs with the gun that hurt like hell. Luckily there was enough charge for the iPod to boot up. I opened the photos folder found the shot and showed him.

He snatched it out of my hand and even though I sensed it coming, I wasn't quick enough to dodge the brutal smack across the jaw with the pistol – the lights went out.

When I revived from that dark place, it felt like I'd been trampled by a herd of Buffalo. There was hardly a part of me that wasn't aching. I struggled up from the bedroom floor, and checked the time on my bedside clock … it was 6 a.m. I'd been out cold all bloody night. Jazz hadn't come in to wake me so either she was being thoughtful or they'd kidnapped her. When I staggered out into the living room I found the latter to be correct. There wasn't much I could do at that hour so I went back into the bedroom and collapsed on the bed.

Sunlight streaming in the window from the living room woke me at 9.20 a.m. I dragged myself into the bathroom and took a quick shower hoping it would make me feel a bit better – it didn't.

I vaguely remembered checking earlier that Jazz wasn't on the lounge and she'd been taken. My face was too sore to shave, my ribs aching so much I couldn't even dry myself properly … but at least I was still alive.

I rang Rick and filled him in. He told me to stay put and not to touch anything, he warned that the case was getting ugly.

I needed a coffee badly so I went into the kitchen, grabbed a carton of milk from the fridge and took a swig, it was thick like yogurt … sour – gross, I nearly threw up. That took the edge off making coffee, or breakfast, so I went down to Grind café on Sussex Street and had raisin toast and fresh coffee. I rang Ty and told him the bad news. It was the first time I'd heard him go off in a panic. I told him to cool down I was on the case … we'd get Jazz back … Detective Malone was on his way to meet me. He kept on repeating: *they will kill her Axis … these bastards are animals.* That wasn't news to me but I understood his anguish. I finally got him off the phone just as two cop cars pulled up out front.

149

CHAPTER
EIGHTEEN

I went out front of the café to catch Rick.

"Bloody-hell!" he growled with a chuckle. "You look like shit!"

"Yeah, well, imagine how I feel," I rasped.

"Go back into the café and order me a black coffee while I send the boys up to dust your flat. Give me your keycard."

I handed it over and went back in the café.

After a while Rick came and sat down.

"Pretty rugged case this one, old son," he announced before I had time to open my mouth.

"Yeah, my fee will go in cosmetic surgery if this keeps up."

"Did you get a look at them?"

"There were three ... Chinese with brown stockings over the heads. I reckon one of them was the guy that clubbed me at the office last week. But I'd never pick them from mug shots if that's what you mean, unless they're all wearing stockings in the photos."

"Glad you've still got your sense of humor," he said with a friendly smile.

"Well, you've gotta laugh, as my Dad used to say. How the fuck did they get Jazz with a guard on her?" I said seriously.

"I've sent DI Parker to her apartment to find that out."

"Should have brought her here. She'd get a laugh out of the state of my face. So what does this do for our case against Grant Lee?"

"Without evidence we've no case, buddy."

"Mate," I grinned at him. "Are you kidding me?"

I knew he was spot on and that didn't make me feel any better. We knew who was behind all of this and the two murders but couldn't prove a damn thing.

"Has Bill been able to turn anything up on him?" I prodded.

"No, the bastard is as clean as a whistle. Too bloody clean, not that that means anything."

"So is he still doing his job?"

"Yeah, but we've got eyes and ears all over him. We even got his cellphone records and found nothing – he must have a specific phone for calling his brother and his gang members."

His phone rang. "Malone ... yes, figured as much. Okay, have 'em dust the place ... don't suppose he got a look at them? Yeah, just like Axis. Okay, see you back at HQ." He put his phone on the table. "That was Parker. She found the guard inside the apartment hogtied and gagged ... No I.D. They had stockings covering their faces."

"What about CCTV in the street?"

"That's Harry's gig. He's onto it. Never know, might get a license plate, but it'd be stolen anyway. Triads are smooth operators, Axis. They rarely leave a clue ... but we've still got to go through the rigors."

"Maybe DI Zhong in Hong Kong can get the cellphone records of the brother's calls, they wouldn't be expecting that," I suggested.

"Good idea, I'll give him a bell. He's a good bloke."

"Saved *my* life," I said with a sigh.

~ ~ ~

Later in my office I was lazing back with my feet up on the desk, doodling on a notepad in my lap racking my brain for clues, when *Someday Soon* chimed in. I answered, "Stone ... Oh, g'day Ty, you have!" I sat up sharply when he said he'd heard from the kidnappers. "Really, okay ... I'll get onto Malone ... no we have to ... what? Listen, after all I've been through that's asking too much ... All right, all right ... I know what comes with the job, it is my business isn't it? You're where? Okay, I'll come there now." After finishing the call I immediately rang Rick. "Hi, I just got off the phone from Ty Sun, he's heard from the kidnappers. They want a signed deal for a majority share in the Golden Dragon and two hundred grand in cash ... No they specifically said no cops or Jazz dies ... he bloody-well wants *me* to do the exchange. Mate, even if I was feeling my best I'd be nervous about it ... No, he wants me to meet him at the Golden Dragon now ... Where's Grant Lee? In his office ... hmm, okay Zhong's onto it, good ... okay, see you there."

I hung up. At least Zhong was able to access Lee's phone records in Hong Kong. I had to hope he'd turn up Grant Lee's Sydney number so we could get his phone log.

~ ~ ~

The sunny day lifted my spirits some on the short walk to the Golden Dragon in Dixon Street. The receptionist gave me a big buck-toothed smile and pointed me at the back room. I joined Rick and Ty at the table.

"Gentlemen, anything further?" I asked urgently.

"Yes, we lifted prints from Miss Sun's apartment and yours – when Parker ran them through AFIS she got a match on a print from Miss Sun's apartment: Fang Peng Jian. He's got form, did two years for possession of an unlicensed firearm."

"Have you heard of him, Ty?"

"No," he said gruffly.

"I got uniforms going with Parker to his apartment in Newtown. Got her a warrant under the terrorism act."

"Handy," I observed.

"Yeah, one thing good that's come out of all the crap in the Middle East. At least we don't lose time now getting warrants."

"How are we going to get my daughter back?" Ty growled impatiently.

"You give Axis two hundred large, he hooks up to make the trade, and we grab them," Rick said.

"And as soon as they sense cops they'll kill her," he growled furiously, and then glowered at me.

"They won't know what hit them. I plan on using our friend Lee Kit Wo, alias Detective Sergeant Grant Lee, to set it up," Rick said.

"How will you do that?" I asked.

"He's got no idea we're onto him, if we can get his phone number from Hong Kong," he held up crossed fingers. "We'll be able to give him the opportunity to join his mates and then track his phone to lead us to them.

"So you are depending on someone in Hong Kong to get his number?" Ty said, his tone lacking any confidence.

"It's all we've got, Ty, unless you have a better plan?" I said.

"No, the only alternative is to give them what they want and then deal with it later," Ty said.

"You'd be risking the lives of Jazz and Axis if you do that. Besides, what makes you think they won't just keep asking for more?" Rick posed.

"My bet is the two hundred grand is something they've dreamed up here because it wasn't part of the deal we did in Hong Kong. They want two-million, but that's after the share transfer."

"That makes sense, besides two-hundred grand isn't enough money for a kidnapping," Rick said.

"So you think brothers Lee are not acting in accord?" Ty asked me.

"Not sure. It might be that the kidnappers are after the money and Grant Lee mightn't even know they've asked for it," I urged.

"Remember, he's under watch in his office at police HQ. For all intents and purposes he just might have ordered for documents only to be exchanged knowing the two mill comes next," Rick considered.

"So if you assume that, then you also assume discord among their ranks and that's why you think this is a more dangerous situation than maybe even Grant Lee thinks it is," Ty summarized.

"Exactly," Rick said.

"I'll tell you what, if the exchange is on a bloody boat I'm not doing it," I complained.

"Why, what have you got against boats?" Ty asked.

"Plenty," I grumbled.

"Where are you up to with the share certificate Mr. Sun? Rick asked.

"My accountant is at ASIC getting the transfer notarized."

"And the money?" I questioned.

"The HSBC will deliver it here soon. Then what happens?" Ty asked.

"We're banking on Zhong getting back to us with Lee's number so that we can put things in place for when we get the exchange time and location from the kidnappers," Rick said.

"So it's a gamble then?" Ty observed.

"It sure is," Rick agreed.

I figured Ty liked the idea of it being a gamble – punters are like that. For me I don't gamble on anything, not even a lottery ticket. It's a mug's game. Any dough I earn is from putting my neck on the line, so I'm not about to give it away cheaply, especially to bloody bookies. I've had too many customers in the racing game for me to believe any sport is on the level any more. It was okay when I was growing up, athletes played sport for honor ... the horses we're "as" rigged then, and far fewer sports enhancement drugs were around but now there's just so much gambling, you can bet on just about anything at anytime, anywhere in the world online. Gambling has corrupted sport in my book and that's just another one of those things in life that pisses me right off.

Rick's phone rang. It was Parker ... there was someone at Fang's Newtown apartment ... she wanted the green light to go in. But Rick wasn't ready ... he ordered a continued stakeout until he was. We were playing the waiting game and it was nerve-racking.

My stomach was beginning to growl for food when

Rick's phone rang again, this time it was Zhong and we were in luck, Lee Kok Lung's phone records showed twenty numbers in Sydney and one he called almost daily. Zhong had faxed the entire phone log to Rick's office. Our spirits had lifted things were beginning to flow our way. Rick phoned Parker and had her check the numbers with the Telco's. Though it was likely Grant would be using a pre-paid chip to avoid detection, it was still worth a try.

"So we have to decide whether to roll the dice on this number your Dragon Head buddy in Hong Kong calls … hoping it belongs to Grant Lee, because we've got no way of confirming it. Our entire plan will be riding on that number. So, it's your call Mr. Sun," Rick outlined.

"Tell me the last three digits of the phone number?" he asked.

"Triple four," Rick replied with a frown.

"Four is a Triad number from ancient times … it signifies the member's position in the organization and the four oceans that surround China and ultimately, the universe," Ty explained.

"What do you mean the member's position?"

"A Dragon Head is triple four," he said with a wry smile.

"We've got him!" Rick said excitedly. "Now we'll put phase one of the operation into motion."

CHAPTER
NINETEEN

Rick rang Parker and had her put a GPS tracker on the number he was banking on to be Grant Lee's sly phone. Then he phoned Bill Rogers at vice and told him to give Grant Lee couple of days off work and to make the excuse plausible. The trap was set ... all we needed was to spring it and wait for the kidnappers to phone Ty with the exchange details. Then for Grant to pay his mates a visit.

One of Ty's bodyguards came in and told him something in Cantonese. Ty gave him an order, which sent him back outside.

"The money has arrived," Ty declared.

The big guy returned carrying a briefcase, handed it to Ty and then left. Ty put it on the table and opened it. The money was in twenty neat ten thousand dollar stacks. Ty read a note left inside the case by the HSBC branch manager.

"The bag has a concealed GPS and some of the notes have micro dot locators," he said, and then picked up a cellphone from the briefcase. "The phone is fitted with a tracking app for the briefcase and the notes."

"Very professional," Rick said.

Ty handed me the cellphone and then locked the case.

I booted it up and opened the app, it showed on a

Google Earth map that the bag and the money were at the Golden Dragon in Dixon Street. It even showed a schematic of the building and exactly where the items were located within.

"How's that?" I said, showing Rick.

"Clever, very clever indeed," he accepted. "I need to get back to the office to coordinate the stakeout in Newtown. Do you need me for anything more here?"

"No, once we've got the call I'll let you know and we can hammer out an exchange strategy," I peeled off.

Ty sighed deeply, "Why haven't they called?"

"You'll have to be patient, Mr. Sun," Rick said. "It'll happen ... Axis is experienced with abductions, he did a great job solving one in the Philippines only a month or so ago."

"Let's just relax and have something to eat," I suggested.

"Okay, talk to you when you've got something ... catch you later," Rick said in a manner oozing confidence.

As soon as Rick had closed the door behind him Ty spoke his mind.

"I have never been one for trusting the police, that is why I hired you, Axis, and now it seems we are at their mercy."

"Had your daughter not been kidnapped, we wouldn't be faced with this situation, Ty," I countered.

"Had the police done their job in the first place she wouldn't have been abducted ... Ah? I rest my case."

"I guess you're right," I said with a shrug. "But you have to agree we have no option, not if you care about the welfare of Jazz."

"That goes without saying, but I'm not sure I'm willing to risk her life on a gamble that the police will be successful, they have nothing to lose you see, unlike you and I ... Did the police solve your kidnapping in the Philippines?"

"No, but I used them when necessary."

"Ah, now we are getting somewhere."

Over lunch we discussed the probable outcomes of the kidnapping. We identified the best possible scenario and agreed to put it into action.

A little while later Ty's phone rang. We sprang into action in case it was the kidnappers, but no, I could tell by his mood swing and him speaking English that it was someone else.

When he finished he said, "That was my accountant, the share certificates transfers are official, fifty one percent of equity in the Golden Dragon is now owned by Lee Kok Lung. Once he has a copy of the certificate in his possession, he can at his leisure call an extraordinary meeting of the board of directors and because he has the majority vote, appoint a new CEO to replace me. I will then be demoted to managing director."

"Because you are the only other director does he have two votes?"

"That's correct."

"You know I had the opportunity to put this straight months ago and didn't," he admitted.

"How's that?"

"A few months ago Chiang got caught up in something ... I may as well be upfront with you he was trafficking drugs. You know that because you saw the photo of him with Grant Lee and the drugs. Well, that was only half of it.

First of all Rosy was a plant by me."

"What?" The divulgence bowled me over.

"Her family owed me for giving her a job at the restaurant, Chiang fancied her, so I got payback by getting her to spy on him ... just to keep track of what he was doing mind you ... He would tell me nothing about what he was up to you understand ... a loose cannon."

"Wait a second, so Rosy took that photo for you? What were you going to do with it?" I asked carefully.

"I was going to use it to blackmail whoever Chiang was dealing with at Sun Yee On into dropping my gambling debt. As it turned out I heard the guy in the photo was a cop, so I dropped the idea ... never even sighted the photo, Rosy just told me she had it," he said with an expressionless voice.

"So your put down of Rosy in front of Jazz was a ruse because she was undercover for you?"

"That's right. I regret she had to die and in that way," he shook his head shamefully.

"If you'd spoken up earlier we might have saved her life," I snapped angrily.

"You're right I know, but sometimes the less said the better."

I took a deep breath to stop me clouting him. "Not when people are risking their lives for you Ty," I growled in a scornful voice.

"Yes, yes, I know you are right."

"I don't care what nationality you are. It's all about trust ... and now I think you should learn to ..." *Someday Soon* started up and distracted me.

"Hey, Rick, what's up? Yeah, I'm thinking of wrapping

here as well ... we can all stay on alert by phone. You will? Okay, that's good. Later," I hung up.

"Rick said the stakeout in Newtown will continue overnight ... and Grant Lee left the office and went to his Maroubra Beach apartment ... he's still there ... DS Parker will monitor Lee twenty four seven. Rick's got a meeting with the Commissioner now, and will go home after that ... he'll only be a phone call away. I think I might go do a couple of things and then head home myself," I said standing, a little despondent.

Ty held out a tentative hand to shake, "I do trust you, Axis, as much as I trust Nick, and you know that he's like a brother."

He pulled me to him and we hugged. It was the first sign to true emotion I'd felt from him.

"Okay, call me as soon as you hear from them. I'll only be ten, fifteen minutes away. Don't worry Ty, this will all turn out positive. Keep your eye on that briefcase."

"Thank you Axis."

I suspected a hint of tears welling up in his tired eyes.

~ ~ ~

What I needed most was to stock up on food, the cupboard was bare. The nearest supermarket was Woolworths Haymarket only ten minutes walk from the restaurant. It was peak hour and I didn't mind battling the hurried pedestrians on the sidewalk.

I'd forgotten about my ribs and by the time I got to my apartment with all the shopping bags, I was in agony. It took a couple of painkillers with three fingers of JD neat to do the trick. Free of pain, I turned on the TV and watched the news. *Someday Soon* woke me from a deep sleep. It was

Nick ... I muted the TV and put him on speaker.

"Hey buddy, how goes it?"

"Good, how are your aches and pains?"

"On the improve."

"Ty called just now and filled me in, good that Zhong got the number..."

"Yeah, let's hope it's the right one, we've got a lot riding on it."

"The old fella seems to be handling it," Nick said.

"He's one tough old goat ... yeah, I was worried about him at first but he's a realist ... sounds hypocritical but he's a smart punter as well."

"I don't know about that Axis, he did run up a hefty gambling debt, so he might not be that smart."

"I hear you ... well we've had to take a punt with this one but you know, I just don't get why dudes as clued up as these Triads would be asking for two hundred grand cash ... along with the share certificate. They'd have to know the notes would be marked wouldn't they?"

"Ty said you think the kidnappers are working apart from Grant Lee, that might explain it. They're probably in for a quick buck and haven't the brains to have thought it through. There'll be hell to pay when the Dragon Head finds out."

"Yeah, it'll be interesting to see how that plays out."

"Don't expect it to, I reckon he'll find out and change the ransom, that might be why it's taking so long for them to get back with the exchange details."

"Old territory mate," I said with a chuckle. "I hope it doesn't go like the last one with the demand not being paid and all hell breaking loose."

"Are you ever going to let me live that down?"

"Nope," I said jokingly.

"Here, someone wants to speak to you ..."

I heard a rustle as he handed the phone to someone.

"Hello stranger ..." a soft female voice purred.

I recognized it immediately.

"Well if it isn't my lovely suicide blonde ... how are you, Lola? I bet you really miss me."

"Only when I'm in bed."

"Oh shucks, I bet you say that to all the fellas," I jested.

"When are you coming up to see me or should I say when will you see me coming?"

"You are a naughty girl ... and I love it! I will be there as soon as I've got this case boxed, I promise."

I immediately thought of Suzie waiting for me at Nick's place in Manila, and Jazz, with her lovely legs and feet. Boy, was I in demand I kidded myself.

"Okay, I'll keep you to your promise Mr. Happy, you be good now and don't go getting hurt."

If only she knew the state of me I thought.

"Okay baby, kiss, kiss ... "

"Bye for now sweetie."

There was a rustle again and Nick came back on line, "I think she misses you mate."

"Her and the rest ... I'll call you when I've got this done."

"Good luck, are you sure you can handle this without me Kemo Sabe?"

"Yes Tonto, but for now it's Hi Yo Silver away!"

~ ~ ~

Someday Soon woke me at 7 a.m. It was Ty, the kidnappers had made contact at 6 a.m. they'd given him a time and instructions. Nick had been right about the ransom changing – it had. I agreed to meet him at my office at 8.30 to talk it through.

I felt revitalized after a good nights sleep. I called into The Grind Café and picked up a coffee to go and then strutted my stuff, bathed in sunlight, to my office building and took the elevator up. I sat behind the desk and after lacing my coffee with a shot of bourbon drank it down – that got the day going. If I'd used whiskey it would be called an Irish coffee but with bourbon I wondered: is it a Kentucky Coffee?

I thought it was about time to get my email ... I hadn't collected it since I started the case. I'd just booted up my Mac when there was a knock at the door. I opened it to Ty.

"Are you all right, you look flustered? Pull up a chair," I said.

"I haven't slept Axis, I need a drink," he gasped.

I poured him a slug of bourbon and handed it to him.

He tasted it and screwed up his nose. "Yuck, what's that?"

"Bourbon, sorry, it's all I've got ... an acquired taste I suppose."

He skulled it anyway and then held out his glass for more. I obliged.

"So tell me what he said?"

"They changed the demand ... I guess it was like you and DI Malone thought, when the Dragon Head found out they'd asked for cash he reacted ... so now they're asking for two million to be paid into an account they'll specify. Once they have the money and the share certificate they will return Jazz."

"That's what's happened all right. Okay, so the first thing to do is ring Rick and tell him about the change of plans. Then to check Grant Lee's movements overnight, and the results of the stakeout."

CHAPTER
TWENTY

The bourbon had returned the color to Ty's face. He nodded for me to continue, so I rang Rick.

He was in the middle of plotting Grant Lee's movements on his office murder board. He asked us both to come to his office to talk but Ty said no, he was afraid that being seen might cause problems for Jazz. Rick agreed, said he'd get a printout of the murder board and come to my office.

We didn't have to wait long before he and Parker arrived. After introducing DS Parker to Ty, we sat around the coffee table peering at the printout from the murder board. It showed Grant Lee's movements as defined by tracking his cellphone.

Rick explained, "We're glad it's the right phone number, checking the address confirmed that. He left the office at 1.30 and proceeded directly to his Maroubra Beach apartment.

Parker gave us some background. "Lee lives alone in a three bedroom penthouse apartment on Marine Parade, Maroubra Beach."

Rick continued. "At 1930 he left his apartment and proceeded to the Fortune Garden Restaurant. Then at 2100 he drove to an office block on Thomas Street, Ultimo, we believe it to be his office and or the offices of Sun Yee On.

He made three phone calls from there. First was to a silent number, probably a pre paid, which there wasn't enough call time to triangulate. The second was international to Hong Kong, a number we identified as belonging to his brother Lee Kook Lung. And the third to the same prepaid, but this time we managed to triangulate it to the general area of Huntley Street, Alexandria. After what we know now, we read this as him first speaking to the kidnappers ... he finds out they've asked for cash, calls his brother and then calls the kidnappers back with the changed plan."

"What time was the last call made?" Ty asked.

Parker checked her records, "It was 05.17 this morning."

"I got the call from them at 6 a.m. so that adds up, doesn't it?" Ty said.

"Sure does," I said enthusiastically. "And what with the stakeout?"

"No one has gone in or out of the Newtown apartment. Which tells us Fang Peng Jian hasn't been home," Parker said.

She crossed her long legs and the move caught my eye. Underneath those thick horrid brown stocking of hers was hidden a pair of shapely legs. In fact underneath that navy blue shirt, light blue blouse and navy jacket I figured dwelt a very sexy body indeed. I wondered if she had a shaved pussy or not when she caught me looking and rolled her eyes impatiently. I expect had Ty not been there she would have given me a pay out for mentally undressing her.

"So what are the new demands, Mr. Sun?" Rick asked.

"They want two-million sent to an account they will specify and the share transfer certificate. He'll text the account number at midday. Once the money is in the account I will get the final instructions for the safe return of Jazz."

"Do you have that sort of money, Mr. Sun?"

"No."

"Can you arrange it?"

"Yes, the bank will loan it to me against the Golden Dragon but with the shares having been transferred they might not."

"Can you find out please?" Rick asked.

"Give your accountant a call," I told him.

Ty nodded, got up and moved away for some privacy to make the call.

"You realize once he makes the transfer it's gone, he won't be able to get it back?" I said. "I went through a similar scenario on the Kitty Lovejoy kidnapping in Manila."

"It comes down to whether Mr. Sun wants to put his daughter's life at risk by us going in with guns blazing," Rick said slowly.

"It's not like he doesn't owe the money. It is a gambling debt isn't it?" Parker observed.

"Yes, it is. He would need something from Fortune Garden to confirm the debt is wiped," I suggested.

"They won't do that it would make them complicit in the kidnapping," Rick said.

Ty returned and sat down. His mouth worked formlessly for a short time, until the words came out with jarring abruptness, "It can be done, but it will mean mortgaging my home, business and Jazz's apartment."

I could see in his eyes it was killing him but Parker was

right, he'd got himself into the fix, he owed the money, what was illegal was the crooks using extortion to get it back.

"Okay, here's the scoop. Ty will pay the money when he gets the account number. Then when they ring with the drop off, I'll take the original share transfer certificate with me to exchange for Jazz. How do you want to fit in with that Rick?"

"Well, we need to get Grant Lee to be there or actually make the exchange otherwise we'll only be able to arrest the others."

"He's unlikely to put himself in that position now that he's got the only evidence, the photo," I said.

"But what about when he ultimately takes a seat on the Golden Dragon board, won't that be enough to arrest him?" Ty pressed.

"I'm afraid not, Ty. I think you'll find you'll be sending the money off shore, so we'll have nothing to tie it to him, as for the share certificate it is in the name of his brother and I expect he will appoint Grant CEO, so there's nothing illegal about that either ... no, the only way we can get him is in direct relation to the kidnapping."

"Damn losing that photo. We had the bastard!" I growled.

"What if Ty was to insist the exchange had to be with the Dragon Head?" Parker suggested.

"No that wouldn't work," I said.

"No, wait a minute, she might have something there," Ty asserted. "What if I needed the Dragon Head to sign a receipt for the share certificate and the debt?"

"That might be worth a try," I said smiling at Parker acknowledging her idea.

Rick stood up and Parker followed. "Okay, we'll wait to hear from you next."

"Will you be keeping an eye on the Newtown apartment?" I asked.

"Yes, and Grant's movements ... I'll put a SWAT team on standby for the handover."

After they'd left, Ty looked me sternly in the eyes and said, "Axis, I don't want a SWAT team going in. It's too big a risk."

"Okay, let's make that decision once we have the location."

~ ~ ~

I walked with Ty to the Golden Dragon and when we reached it he asked me inside for Yum Cha, which I duly accepted. I'd grown to like dim sum. It was a full house and as we walked through the restaurant, squeezing past busy waiters, I noticed a customer with a familiar face. I let it go and continued on to the private room.

While Ty was ordering the penny suddenly dropped ... I jumped up so quickly I frightened him, "What's up?" He demanded.

"I just realized who's sitting outside in your restaurant," I barked.

"Who?"

"Bloody Fatty Tung, that's who, the Sun Yee On enforcer, the red pole, he should be in jail!"

"That has to be more than just a coincidence. Where are you going?" he asked as I was moving off.

"To shirt-front him."

"Be careful," he yelled after me and then growled something in Chinese.

As I came out into the restaurant I suddenly realized Ty's henchmen were following me. I walked up to Tung and glared down at him.

"Well take a look at what the cat dragged in, if it isn't Mr. Red Pole, Fatty enforcer Tung. Tell me," I said sarcastically leaning on the back of his chair, "what brings you to Sydney? Wait, even more important than that, how the hell did you get out of jail in Hong Kong?"

That was for the benefit of his associates in case they didn't know. Tung glared up at me. I watched his expression change when he sighted the bookends standing behind me.

"Stone, you are a very irritating person ... has anyone told you that?" he snarled.

"Plenty, especially while they're being carted off to prison," I replied caustically.

"Can't a man travel to Sydney for business without some two-bit Aussie PI sticking his nose in where it does not belong?" he countered.

"We'll see about that Tung, I know you're *business* here, I warn you ... don't get in my way, this isn't Hong Kong ... you're now on my turf."

I gave him a death stare and didn't pay him the courtesy of making a reply. I turned on my heel for my escort to walk me back to the private room.

~ ~ ~

I sat down opposite Ty and said uneasily, "Tung being here is not a good omen. Do you know what the Red Pole does in the organization?"

"No, but you're going to tell me."

"The Dragon Head sets policy and the Red Pole enforces it, without question."

"That mean Soy was overstepping his job as White Paper Fan wanting to bump me off, wouldn't that have been Tung's job?"

"Yes, though not necessarily for him to do it personally but certainly to organize the hit. Soy must have had serious reasons to want to shoot you."

I knew the reason but had no intention of telling him I'd been bonking Soy's girlfriend. There were bigger issues.

"His presence raises questions, what's he here for? Is he to play a role in the kidnapping handover or is he here as eyes and ears for the Dragon Head because he doesn't trust his younger brother?" I proposed.

"These are good questions. I suggest the last question answers itself. I think that would be the only reason for him being here. I expect Grant Lee would be trying to complete the task without interference from Hong Kong. Pride is often the driving force with Chinese people."

"That makes perfect sense Ty."

"I hope you didn't challenge Tung in front of his associates or he will be forced to retaliate out of pride."

"Hmm, well, we might have an issue there."

~ ~ ~

When I left the restaurant Tung was nowhere to be seen. I headed for the office. *Someday Soon* sounded just as I was entering the building. I stopped and took the call.

"Stone, who's calling?"

"You don't need to know my name, but I can tell you this … he is here to kill you. You know who I am talking about."

"The Red Pole?"

"I can say no more, I'm just warning you. Goodbye, Mr.

Stone. Good luck."

He terminated the call. There was no number ... he sounded Asian but with an Aussie accent. Who could it be and why warn me? Whatever the case I now had to watch my back.

I decided against going up to the office, I'd been caught there once before. I'd left my .38 at home, I would feel more comfortable carrying it, so I headed there. Along the way I rang Rick and filled him in on Fatty Tung being in town and getting the warning. He figured the two were connected and it might have one of the guys at the table. I asked if Grant Lee had been on the move, like to the airport perhaps to collect Tung. But no, he had been at his apartment all morning and made no more calls on his sly phone. I suggested he might not know Tung is in town. Rick said he would have someone check all the airport arrival manifests from incoming flights originating in Hong Kong and the immigration records, over the last forty-eight hours. Once he can finger him, he'll check arrivals CCTV footage to see who met him. I let him get on with it.

~ ~ ~

I got myself a neat JD to ease the pain, it being my preferred medicine. On the couch with my feet on the coffee table, I unraveled my pistol cleaning kit on my lap. It had been a while since I'd serviced the .38, I figured it should be running to perfection just in case it was called upon to save my ass. A little music wouldn't go astray so I grabbed the remote and triggered the CD player not knowing what was loaded ... I recognized the album from the first note of the first track *Cluster One* ... Pink Floyd's *Division Bell*. It was good music for what I was doing but when the second track

What Do You Want from Me started up, the lyric sounded personal. It seemed like the lyrics were reiterating the threat from Fatty Tung: *"Do you want my blood – what do you want?* I knew it was all in my mind, but at the same time, I have this thing about omens. In Brisbane many years ago I met a girl named Vanessa, we had amazing sex: a one-night-stand. As it turned out she was a practicing white witch. In parting she warned me not to drive on a certain day. I thought nothing of it but on that particular day, in Sydney, I decided to drive somewhere – I had a terrible car accident that could have killed me – it didn't because I was almost expecting it to happen thanks to her. She'd taught me to listen to my conscience and pay heed to omens. Call me old-fashioned but I've always maintained that saying you don't believe in superstition is being *superstitious*. So, I tuned the CD player off before any more lyrics could get to me.

CHAPTER
TWENTY-ONE

"Not another kidnapping!" Lola said. "Just open your pants and I'll take care of it."

I touched her glory hole; it was still wet with my saliva. I opened my pants and released Mr. Happy. He was as hard as a rock. I held him and stroked him to get him harder.

I woke with a start holding the barrel of my .38 – I must have nodded off. What a dream I was having ... I needed another JD. Sometimes I wonder if there's ever anything else on my mind than pussy. I'm obsessed with it, why?

It was quarter of six and getting dark. I turned on the lights and poured myself a fresh JD. It wasn't like me to sleep during the day ... sleeping-in during the morning sure, I was a night owl and it came with the territory – though my mother always said that because I was born at 4 a.m. I was a night person and condemned to the realm of vampires, sinister nightlife and the pool halls of life, forever.

The evening dragged on. I cooked steak eggs and fries for dinner ... polished off a few more JD's and watched a movie on cable that was about as memorable as the photograph of a toothbrush. Close to midnight I was tempted to ring Ty, I knew he'd be up but decided not to, it could all wait until tomorrow. With my companion parked within reach I curled up in bed with a book.

A protesting bladder woke me at 7 a.m. I'd had enough sleep for a month anyway, so I put the TV on and made a pot of coffee and some burnt toast.

By half eight, I was all spruced up ready to go when *Someday Soon* kick started the day.

"Stone ... Hi, Rick, what's doing?"

"I need you in here."

He had his grumpy head on.

"What's the problem? You don't sound too friendly."

"Do I always have to sound friendly, Axis?" he grated.

"No, I guess not ... it was just an observation."

"Look, I've spent the last hour being hauled over the coals by the boss, now he wants to speak to you."

"Oh, shit. Nothing worse than Humpty Dumpty wanting to stick his fuckin' nose into a case I'm on, you know how much he hates me ... or should I say every bloody PI in the business," I snarled.

"Yes, I know Donald is intolerant of PI's, but unfortunately this time he's got a case."

"Fill me in."

"No, I'll let him do that. Come down to my office once you've been upstairs. He's expecting you at 9.30."

"All right, I'll hit the frog and toad now, catch you there," I signed off.

Superintendent Humphrey Donald, whom I'd nicknamed Humpty Dumpty because he was half the size of a bus, couldn't stand the sight of me. We had a history of face-offs over the last ten years and I wasn't looking forward to this one. Normally I could count on Rick for support but it seemed that wasn't going to be the case this time. I decided to change into something more suitable for the meeting, so I dusted down my only gray suit, dug out my only necktie, unearthed a nearly clean white shirt and decked myself out. I even found my old leather briefcase under a pile of porn magazines, so I rubbed the mildew off it and then cruised downstairs feeling pretty good about myself. Didn't take long to catch a cab to police HQ in Surry Hills.

~ ~ ~

I checked my reflection in the closed polished-steel elevator doors on my way up to the headmaster's office. That's how it felt: I'd been summoned.

I entered his domain and fronted his haggard secretary. She had the personality of an armpit with looks like something the cat had dragged in.

"Good-morning Miss Carpin, I'm here to see the Superintendent."

"Take a seat, Mr. Stone, he will see you when he's good and ready," she said as dull as dishwater.

"Where would you like me to take it," I joked just to piss her off. She stared blankly at me, didn't get it. I sat down and mumbled under my breath just loud enough for her to hear, "Well, some people have a sense of humor."

I'd counted the carpet tiles on the floor, read Women's Weekly and picked all the lint off my suit jacket by the time I was ushered into his office.

I sat in the sole chair positioned in front of his desk and waited for the huge double-chinned lump of a man to look up from what he was reading and acknowledge my existence. When that didn't happen I decided to speak up.

"Good morning, sir!" I'd figured to raise my voice a little above the normal, so he'd have no chance of pretending he didn't hear me. Only somewhere along the way I made a miscalculation and my voice erupted into the room in one great volcanic blast of sound that could have awakened the dead. But got the desired result, he looked up and over his small round wire frame glasses and scowled at me.

"Stone," he grumbled distastefully. He peeled off his glasses for added impact and held up the paper he'd been reading. "This is a report of the Sun kidnapping signed off by Inspector Malone, it doesn't mention you ... until the most important part, the handover ... of which Malone seems under the delusion you are in control. So I asked myself, when I go to the commissioner to explain why we've laid off an officer, Detective Grant Lee, held a twenty-four seven stakeout on a Newtown apartment, spent a fortune on technology surveillance - do I tell him it was all for Axis Stone so he could get paid his fee!"

"Oh, I think there's a little more to it than that superintendent," I countered. "You wouldn't have a case if I hadn't brought it to you. You department was wading around with sharks in a pond studying a dead leg without a clue until I cracked the case open for you ... so is this what I get in thanks, some sort of schoolboy dressing down from you?"

"Your impertinence is legendary Stone, I remind you it is your duty as a citizen to bring to police information of a crime that might lead to a conviction!"

"I am a licensed private detective Superintendent Donald, and that license gives me the right to operate within the law and act for clients who aren't being satisfied by the police system."

There's no ham like a big ham. The Superintendent

proved it with the most elaborate double take I'd seen in ages. And then he exploded.

"Don't you read the letter of the law to me boy!"

"Look sir, you can build your blood pressure up another five points by bawling me out but that isn't going to get us anywhere. I act for Mr. Ty Sun, it is his daughter that has been kidnapped, it is my job to get her back safely and I am working with your office to facilitate such. If you don't like it, then that's your problem, to be frank, we have bigger problems than that on our hands and all this crap is just slowing us down ... now, ask me a question and I'll give you an answer and if that helps you with the Commissioner then good, but let me make this clear - nothing will distract me from doing my job on this case."

"Be that as it may Stone, you will have to tow the line with the police. I understand it is on your say-so that DI Malone has had DI Bill Rogers lay off DS Lee but when I asked for a reason, none was forthcoming."

"So is that what this is all about? Why didn't you just say that in the first place?" I said stiffly.

I realized the problem and it was a sticky one. Rick obviously hadn't told Humpty of our suspicion that Lee was the local Dragon Head of Sun Yee On. He couldn't run the risk. I had to think of what to say to settle the situation. Rick must be hoping I could save the day. I had an idea.

"Look, I was in Hong Kong a few days ago working with the Hong Kong Police in connection to the possible involvement of a Triad organized crime ring called the Sun Yee On in this case. After meeting with the leaders of the Sun Yee On, one of them tried to shoot me and was shot dead by police. The leader is Lee Kok Lung who we believe to be the older brother of DS Grant Lee. That being the case, to avoid a conflict of interest, it was decided by your people to keep this confidential and have DS Grant Lee kept clear of the case until the allegations can be substantiated. Does that make sense?"

A pregnant pause followed while he digested all I'd said.

"I suppose so," he eventually mumbled in a derisive voice.

I'd beaten him and couldn't help but smile. "Will there be anything else, sir?"

"No, thank you for coming in Stone," he said with an expressionless voice. Then he put his glasses back on and looked down at his paperwork. I'd been dismissed.

~ ~ ~

I certainly caught the attention of Parker when I cruised into Rick's office in my best threads.

"Well, will you look at fancy pants. Where's the funeral?" she sneered.

"Merely garbed up to do your job for you, calming the bureaucratic storm so to speak," I gloated.

"So what did you tell Donald?" Rick asked with interest.

"It was all about Grant Lee wasn't it? So I told him the Hong Kong cops suspect he's the brother of Lee Kok Lung, Dragon Head of the Sun Yee On in Hong Kong and until that can be substantiated we agreed to keep him at arms length, for his benefit as much as anything else."

"Well done!" Rick beamed at me.

Even Parker was forced to raise a single eyebrow and a nod of approval.

Rick stood up from behind his desk, "Well, if you look here I can throw some light on Mr. Fatty Tung." He swiveled his computer monitor around for me to view. It was CCTV of Sydney International airport arrivals. A number of arriving travellers were wheeling their bags out from behind a partition to be met by friends or relatives.

Rick pointed to the screen, "Here comes Fatty," he said like it was a game show. "Note he's not carrying a suitcase."

Fatty strolled out and was met by two Chinese businessmen in suits.

Rick zoomed the picture and then froze it. "The one on the left is Jacky Chan, no not the actor, but the managing director of the Fortune Garden restaurant. The bloke on the right is Diamond Liu, manager of the Fortune Garden mahjong room. We had them in last week when we busted the casino."

"Yep, both of them were with him at the Golden Dragon yesterday. So he arrived yesterday then?" I posed.

"Yes," Parker said.

"He must have gone directly from the airport to the Golden Dragon ... of course the question begs why, when they've got a restaurant of their own?" Rick questioned.

"Must have been to do with the third guy at the table who wasn't at the airport," I surmised.

"What if he's the guy they've chosen to run the Golden Dragon and that's why they met there? What if Grant Lee isn't going to take over like we thought?" Parker suggested.

"I think you've hit the nail right on the head there Parker," I said grinning at her.

"That would make sense, also they might have thought the Fortune Garden was under police surveillance after the bust," Rick added.

"Maybe it was the third guy that rang me with the

warning?" I pondered.

"Why would he do that?" Parker asked.

"When I went off about Fatty getting out of jail to come here, he looked surprised. Maybe he's a businessman that had been roped into the deal and now wants out?"

"Could be," Rick said, holding his chin thinking.

"Hmm, anything on the stakeout Humpty Dumpty was moaning about?" I asked them.

"He always goes off about stakeouts, doesn't like paying overtime," Rick complained.

"Not a soul has come out or entered the place," Parker admitted.

"Didn't you say there was someone in there from the beginning?" I pressed.

"It turned out a false alarm," she said shaking her head disappointedly.

"We can only keep it going another twenty four hours," Rick added.

"Fair enough, I'd expect Ty to hear from them soon."

"Can I interest you in a coffee?" Parker asked. It was the first time she'd asked – things were looking up – I should wear a bag of fruit more often.

"Thanks Parker," I said, with a big Cheshire cat grin.

She waddled off to get them.

"I think she fancies you today Axis," Rick quipped.

"Obviously she's impressed by the threads mate," I said flicking a non-existent scrap of lint off the lapel.

CHAPTER
TWENTY-TWO

"How seriously are you taking the threat on you life?" Parker asked me as we were sipping our coffees.

"Why Parker are you worried about me?" I joked.

There was a wicked glint in her eyes, "More likely the chance of getting rid of you."

"Oh Parker, just when I thought we were becoming friends," I said sarcastically.

Just then *Someday Soon* cranked up. "It's Ty," I said eagerly checking the ID. "Yes Ty, how goes it? Okay, I'll be right over." I pocketed my phone and stood. "He's heard from them."

"Do you want us with you?" Rick said quickly.

"No, let me talk it through with him, he clams up when you're around. I'll call you."

"Okay, good luck," Rick said.

I was half way out the door when Parker called to me, "I was only having you on Stone, I don't want anything to happen to you."

"Thanks Parker, that was almost convincing," I said with a sarcastic chuckle closing the door behind me.

~ ~ ~

I could have walked to the Golden Dragon it would have only taken fifteen minutes but I saw a cab and hailed it. As it turned out we missed a couple of traffic lights and it still took fifteen minutes and cost me eighteen bucks. I got a receipt for expenses – I can't believe the cost of taxis these days.

~ ~ ~

Ty was pacing the floor of the private room when I came in.

"Axis, this is getting more complicated by the minute," he growled.

"Sit down, relax mate," I said helping him into a chair at the table. "Now, tell me why it's getting complicated?"

"The two million has to be in this bank account by noon," he handed me a piece of paper with a long account number scratched on it. "If it's not there they will hurt Jazz."

"Did they mention the share certificate?"

"No, by the look of it they want the money first. I don't think two million can be arranged at such short notice."

"Have you called your accountant yet?"

"No, I was waiting on you."

"Well, this is where you have to make the choice between money and your daughter Ty," I said slowly.

"You make it sound like a game show."

"I'm sorry if you think that but it's a fact. It's eleven ten, you've got forty-five minutes, a digital transfer only takes a couple of minutes – it's your call."

Without hesitation he dialed his cellphone.

"Mr. Singe, the transfer of funds needs to be made at noon. I know its not much time, but I have no control over that ... I will text you the account number and the bank ID. Yes, please confirm when it is done. The bank knows me well enough. Yes I will sign the mortgage whenever that is needed. Thank you Mr. Singe, goodbye." He glanced at me gloomily. "It's done. Now we must play the waiting game again."

He ordered a bottle of bourbon.

"Looks like I've converted you to Kentucky Whiskey."

"Like you said it is an acquired taste. Tell me, are you sure she won't be hurt?"

"I don't know, Ty. It totally depends on the sort of blokes we're dealing with."

"How did it play out in the Philippines?"

"The kidnapper was a corrupt cop with some powerful friends. He had the victim drugged out of her head, tied to a chair on a boat moored in a marina. When we made the exchange she was wired to a bomb set to blow her and me to bits as soon as she was moved. Nick had a technical gadget that jammed the remote triggering signal to the bomb but only for a minute or so. So we had to locate her, cut her free of her bonds, jam the signal and then get the hell out of before the bomb exploded."

"Obviously you were successful."

"The bomb went off and the three of us were very lucky to be far enough away from it to avoid serious injury."

"So was the ransom paid?"

"No, it was Nick's money. He decided at the last moment to call the bluff and rely on technology. The only trouble was he didn't tell me he hadn't paid."

"Would that have made any difference?"

"Probably not, I've got no qualms. He did what he had to do. Unfortunately, this case is different."

"Why is that?"

"We had the location of the victim, and the kidnapper made the mistake of trying to do all things at once: getting the money and getting rid of the victim and me."

"So if we had the location would we be able to pull off a similar thing?" he asked.

"Sure, but I think you need to consider the ramifications. I don't think the Sun Yee On would be very impressed if you stung them ... is ripping them off hereditary or something?"

He chuckled, "It seems so ... no I'm just considering my options. I expect you might soon know the location because it's getting more serious."

"You mean by tracking Grant Lee?"

"Yes."

"I agree with that, I tell you what, if you're willing to risk Jazz and the consequences, then we will we need to delay the transfer of money long enough to get to them," I explained.

"What if I don't send them the full amount, say only two hundred thousand? They would get digital notification that the funds have arrived in the said account, but it would take them maybe twenty-four hours or so before they would know exactly how much they received?" Ty proposed.

"And they will be expecting the full amount, clever. You know that might just work, but it's a gamble."

"How do you think I ran up the debt in the first place," he smiled.

"But you weren't using your daughter's life as collateral," I submitted.

"Fuck it Axis, we do it!" Ty snapped angrily.

"Right. But we're going to need the police on side, do

you agree?"

"Okay, but only up to a point ... I only trust you," he said truthfully.

"I hear you. Okay, let's make the arrangements."

Ty got on the phone to Mr. Singe to change the directions to the bank and I rang Rick to fill him in on everything. Rick reported there had been movement from Grant; he was in his car right now driving towards the airport. Time was ticking. I knew from experience it would all happen in a rush, so we needed to be prepared. Rick put a team on standby. I requested for it not to be SWAT, just three marksmen. He agreed.

We expected the location to be somewhere in the vicinity of Huntley Street, Alexandria where we had picked up Fang's call before. It was a logical choice as there were plenty of disused warehouses in the area, a perfect refuge to be holed up in with a hostage.

As noon approached, so did our anxiety. Our minds filled with doubt, justification, then more doubt. Ty was struggling with having put his only child at risk.

"I gave her a privileged upbringing you know? Her mother died giving birth to her ... the best schools ... never having to want for anything, and now I put all of that at risk for money," he said, with eyes reflecting self doubt.

"I've only known your daughter a short while but in that time I have grown to respect her. Don't feel ashamed for what you're doing Ty, because I assure you she's a chip off the old block, and would do the same if the roles were reversed and you were the kidnap victim."

"You think she will understand?" he said softly.

"I know she will."

He placed a hand on my shoulder and said warmly, "Thank you for saying that Axis."

As soon as the clock ticked over noon Ty's phone rang. It was Mr. Singe confirming the funds had been sent and received.

"My bet is you won't be contacted until tonight ... they'll want to exchange under the cover of darkness."

"An exit strategy?" he posed.

"Yes indeed, they need to hand over Jazz without harming her and without being caught. Rick already has an undercover team in the area we think will be the location."

"What about the share certificate?" he queried.

"You and I both know that it means nothing – anyone could make up a dummy share certificate. No, Lee Kok Lung would already know that his name appears on the ASIC registry as the principal shareholder of the Golden Dragon," I explained.

"He would have accessed that on-line," Ty said knowingly.

"Yep. So once the cash ransom was elbowed, the certificate became a red herring," I suggested.

"For what reason?"

"To buy time ... what intrigues me is if Parker was right and Fatty Tung is in town for the take over, and Grant Lee doesn't know he's here, then there's going to be one hell of a fight over this," I said, indicating the restaurant. "So they will just leave Jazz somewhere and tell us the location, there won't be any hand-over at all."

"You're saying we will get Jazz back ... the threat to you from Tung will stand and when both parties discover they don't have the two million ..."

"Yep, the shit will hit the fan," I smiled knowingly.

"You anticipated this didn't you?" Ty protested.

"I had a fair idea."

"So what is the failsafe plan?"

"First cab off the rank is to get Jazz back safely."

Once again there was no point sitting around at the restaurant waiting for a call that I didn't expect would come until dark, so I decided to go to the nerve center to watch things unfold.

~ ~ ~

It was a nice afternoon for a walk. When I reached the pedestrian crossing on George Street, I was waiting with the crowd for the lights to change when I remembered Mark's story of the blade in the butt and turned my head sharply when I felt someone press against me from behind. I slipped my briefcase behind to cover my ass when I realized I was the only non-Asian in the throng on the sidewalk – it was after all Chinatown, and that fact unnerved me even more. I anticipated the lights changing and darted out in front of the horde and jogged across the wide street. I kept on going like a man on a mission, along Goulburn Street, over Elizabeth Street, across Wentworth Avenue, then Brisbane Street to Police HQ. I arrived in the lobby puffing out of breath and with a protesting ribcage.

Rick thought it was hilarious when I told him about my attack of paranoia at the crossing.

"I didn't have you pictured as the type to panic Axis," he chuckled.

"It's not often a bloke gets a professional executioner threatening to kill him, Rick!" I objected.

"No, I suppose you're right. Anyhow you made it. So

what's your take on it now?" he asked.

"Are the troops in place?"

"Yes, but the kidnappers would have bailed as soon at the money hit the bank. I know because Grant got a call at exactly 12.04 from Hong Kong. It had to be confirmation from his brother."

"Last you told me he was heading for the airport, where did he go from there?"

"He stopped for an hour at Mascot and then drove back home to Maroubra."

"Damn! And the stakeout?" I queried.

"Well we had a bit of luck there, a Chinaman in his mid thirties, short but bulky, dressed in a suit, entered the apartment about fifteen minutes ago. Parker's there to supervise the arrest."

"Well, finally something's going our way."

"How's the old boy feeling about the gamble?"

"Gambling is his livelihood, it was his idea," I reminded him.

"His daughter won't be impressed when she finds out."

"No, she would expect that from him," I admitted.

"You're kidding me? Funny people these Chinese. There's going to be all hell to pay when the bad guys find out they've been short changed."

"When is Grant Lee due back at work?" I asked.

"Tomorrow."

"So we're riding on two hopes right now, first that we're right and Jazz will be dumped somewhere and they'll let us know where in due course and second, Fang Peng Jian is at his apartment and he will blow the whistle."

"Yeah, well I need to make an arrest to balance the

books ... the shark leg case is still outstanding, so we're banking on Fang all right."

"Not good enough for Humpty Dumpty that you get the kidnap victim back unharmed?"

"For some, yes, but for him, no," he shook his head.

CHAPTER
TWENTY-THREE

Parker arrived back at HQ and announced to us she had Fang in remand.

"No hiccups?" Rick enquired.

"No, he answered the door and we cuffed him, hasn't said a word since ... his lips are sealed."

"Well, they'll certainly come unstuck when we get Jazz back to identify him," I said.

"You obviously questioned him about his part in the kidnapping and the whereabouts of the victim?" Rick queried.

"Yes sir, like I said he has said nothing, not a word."

"Okay, we'll give him a while to stew in a cell then we'll interview him."

"No point me hanging around then," I said getting to my feet.

"Oh, I don't know, I quite like you in that suit," Parker said with a cheeky grin.

"If I didn't know you better Parker I'd think you're trying to get into my pants," I suggested gleefully.

"Not the pants Axis, the suit," she returned serve with interest.

"You going to be all right?" Rick asked.

I patted my trusty companion strapped under my right arm. "As long as I'm with my bodyguard I'm okay. I'll call you when I know something. If you get anything of value out of Fang, bell me."

~ ~ ~

Out front of police HQ *Someday Soon* aroused my interest. It was Nick.

"Hey Nick, what's the latest from beautiful downtown Brisbane?"

"I'm ringing to ask you?"

"You know who I bumped into at the Golden Dragon restaurant yesterday? Fatty Tung."

"What the...? Out of jail and in Sydney!"

"And at Ty's restaurant with three other guys, two of them turned out to be Jacky Chan from Fortune Garden and Diamond Liu ..."

"The manager of the mahjong room, yeah I know them both. What the hell would they be doing at the Dragon?"

"I suspect the third guy is the planned successor to Ty as CEO of the restaurant."

"That would make sense but what's that got to do with Fatty Tung?"

"Guess it's more to do with the Hong Kong chapter than the Sydney one ... anyhow, I gave him a bit of stick and he threatened me."

"When are you going to learn to keep your mouth shut mate?"

"I know, I know, sometimes I just can't help myself ... anyhow, that said, the cops have got one of the alleged kidnappers in detention and we're still waiting to learn the location of Jazz."

"How's Ty holding up?" he asked.

"He's fine, I'm on my way to him now from police HQ."

"Watch your back buddy," he warned. "Tung is a ruthless killer."

"Yeah well, I've dealt with a few of them in the past, so I'm feeling confident. What's news with you?"

"Oh, I meant to tell you ... your Suzie Wong got busted at Manila airport with a bullet in her bag."

"What! A Bullet? How's that?" I snapped.

"It's the latest airport scam in Manila. A security official slips a bullet into someone's bag for it to show up on the X-ray machine. Then that person is taken aside by officials and asked for a bribe or charges will be laid."

"Bloody-hell, you Filo's think of some scams don't you? So, what happened?"

"Dom was waiting for her at arrivals to drive her home and after an hour, he started to get worried so he made some enquiries. Luckily he had a friend in customs that happened to be on duty and he managed to fix them up for a few thousand pesos and got Suzie out. She was a bit rattled though."

"Poor kid ... after all she'd been through. Is she all right now?"

"Yes, but she needs to hear from you. You've got my home number there, give her a ring when you get a chance," he suggested.

"I'll do that mate, thanks. I'll call you later once we've got Jazz."

"Cool, if you need me there just yell out and I can be on the next plane."

"Thanks mate."

I hung up seriously glad to have such a good mate in Nick.

~ ~ ~

I got to the Golden Dragon without any problems or worry but Ty wasn't there. I sighted one of his bodyguards and asked where he was and he told me Fortune Garden. I couldn't believe what I was hearing. Of all places, it'd be like entering a lion's den carrying half a side of beef – just asking for it. I rang him.

"Ty, where are you?"

"Axis, I'm having a drink with an old friend."

"Yeah, where?"

"At Fortune Garden."

"Are you crazy?"

"Axis, you worry too much, what's going to happen to me, uh? No one has threatened my life ... all of my friends play mahjong here, it is what we Chinese do."

"Okay, then don't come looking for me if you find trouble there, the two guys with Fatty Tung at your restaurant were Jackie Chan and Diamond Liu, I'd expect you know them?"

"Yes, as a matter of fact Diamond Liu is standing quite near to me now, maybe I should ask him why Fatty Tung is in Sydney. Wait a second ..."

"No! ... Ty ... no! ... for God's sake don't say anything! " But it was too late I could hear him talking in Chinese, it had to be with Liu.

He came back to me. "We go back a long way ... he said Tung is here, like you thought, for the debt settlement and the take over of my restaurant."

"He told you that?" I said surprised.

"Yes, of course, he has nothing to hide. I'll be here for two or three hours, if they call I will ring you straight away, in the meantime go home, get some rest, you sound stressed," he said blithely.

I took his advice and braving it, walked home.

~ ~ ~

It felt good to relax back in my favorite armchair with a JD in hand to just chill. Things had been chaotic – Ty was right – I was stressed. Suzie surged into my mind so I dialed Nick's Fort Bonifacio home. It wasn't an easy call, I was expecting her to be happy to hear from me but all she did was cry. Being emotional made it difficult for her to explain herself in English. It was one of those calls where you try to find a way to end it without causing any more grief. When I tried to say goodbye she just started up again asking when I'd be there with her. When I couldn't give her an answer she burst into tears and so around and around it went, until finally I just said, "Okay baby, kiss kiss ... I'll talk to you soon ... bye," and hung up which left me feeling guilty as sin. It took a couple more JD's before I managed to negotiate the guilt-trip threshold.

The orange glow of sunset radiated in through my lounge room window adding to the warm glow from the JD's.

There was a knock at the door. It opened and a dark-haired, Chinese girl glided across the room toward me. She wore a beautiful, hip-length, Mandarin jacket of green silk with delicate embroidery woven across the front panels, and absent-minded, because she'd forgotten to put on the bottom half of the outfit. I sat up so I could better appreciate the real-life shapeliness of those tapered legs.

She hovered just a few feet from me and said in a husky voice, "Take your pants off."

I quickly slid them and my underpants down to expose Mr. Happy standing erect like a flagpole. Licking her lips she glided up to me and thrust her hand at me pushing me back on the lounge then straddling me. She rose onto her knees and positioned her hot wet sheath ready to take my throbbing sword. I looked into her eyes, they were the color of her jacket, there was something wrong – it can't be Rosy - she'd dead!

She leaned her face close to mine and lowered her pelvis so that the tip of Mr. Happy was just touching the gates of her lust ... then she whispered hoarsely, "I sent you ..."

Suddenly her eyes looked mad ... stark raving mad. She opened her mouth wide like she was about to scream and exposed a mouthful of sinister unearthly pointed teeth and then hissed like a cat. In a panic, I was drawn to look sharply down at Mr. Happy. Suddenly her labia parted and a mouth projected from her vulva like the alien in the movie of the same name, and pointed teeth dripping with saliva gnashed and snapped at my cock like some sort of venomous reptile. Then it struck with the speed of a viper and bit the end clean off my cock.

I screamed and sat up in shock, wide-eyed my heart pounding a like the dance floor of a disco. I looked down, my pants were still on ... it was a fucking dream ... I sighed, then jumped up, strode to the cellarette, poured myself four fingers of JD and skulled it. No more friggin" afternoon catnaps for me!

~ ~ ~

About half an hour later *Someday Soon* shattered the mental image of Rosy the vampire with good news. Ty had been contacted.

"What did they say?" I asked.

"It was a different person than before."

"How do you know?"

"He had a Shanghai accent, the caller before was from Ghangzhou. He said Jazz can be collected … but only by you."

"Me, what they asked for me by name?"

"Yes."

"That's a bit odd isn't it?"

"Yes, I thought so too."

"Okay, so where is she?"

"He said we will find her at 17A Port Access Road, White Bay."

"Rozelle. Whoa! That's a long way from Alexandria where Rick has snipers planted."

"I think that place was … what do you call it, a red herring?"

"Yeah Ty, it seems so," I agreed if not little vaguely.

"Oh, and he said you are to come alone, unarmed."

"Yeah right and pigs fuckin' fly … first of all if I'm just going to collect Jazz, what would it matter if I had an army with me? Secondly, I'm not about to shoot her so if there isn't going to be someone there to shoot me, why should I be unarmed."

"I guess you're right, it must be a trap to get you."

"There's only one person who wants to get square with me and that's Fatty Tung. Jazz mightn't even be there, and if she is, she might be dead."

"No! She's alive I spoke to her."

"Did she tell you anything?"

"Only that he said he will kill her if there are any police."

203

I could feel the noose tightening around my neck. Fatty was gunning for me, now they think they've got the money and the restaurant the hostage is his to lure me.

"All right, did he give you a time?"

"Yes, at 9.30 p.m."

"That only gives me an hour and a half."

"What are you going to do Axis? I didn't hire you to walk into a trap with a gangster where only one will walk away."

"It nearly always comes down to this ... Just leave it to me Ty."

"I'll send Sunny with the car to drive you."

"Who is Sunny?"

"My bodyguard who pulled the knife on you."

"Oh, that's Sunny. Good, tell him to pick me up out front of the Regal Apartments Sussex Street at nine, and tell him he'll have to wait for me and then bring us both back, even if I'm dead. You got that Ty?"

"Yes Axis ... I got it. Good luck."

I rang Rick and told him the change of plan but left out the location. They'd got nothing out of interrogating Fang. The only hope he had left of making him talk was getting Jazz to identify him. When I told him I was going in alone he went off at me big time – but at the end of the day – Fatty had left us no choice. He pleaded for me to give him the location but as much as I'm his friend, I had to deny him – he wasn't pleased with me at all.

I finished the call with, "The next time you hear from me mate it'll be to send a body bag for Fatty Tung."

CHAPTER
TWENTY-FOUR

A cold front had moved in, I could hear the wind howling outside. Winter had arrived. A hip holster would be the wisest choice in the dark, easier to draw and less conspicuous. I strapped it on over my black shirt. The weather outside was angry, I'd need to be rugged up against it, so I pulled my black three quarter length driza-bone coat from the wardrobe and my favorite black Fedora hat. Garbed up I checked myself in the full length mirror – black jeans, black R.M Williams Cuban heel boots – the waterproof coat, the hat – awesome, I was ready to rock. One last thing ... I trawled through my junk draw for a flick-knife ... it was a souvenir from a job a few years back. I found it ... a quick test to satisfy it was still working and I slipped it into my coat pocket.

It was time to head downstairs to meet Sunny. I skulled a JD for some Dutch courage, took a look around my apartment to motivate me that it wouldn't be the last time I'd see it, and bailed out.

It was blowing a gale outside. Sussex Street runs north to south and at this time of year the southerly wind can power through the canyons of the city like a dragons breath. I stayed behind the glass lobby doors out of the elements waiting for Sunny to show. There were few people in the street it was too much of a fight to keep an umbrella from turning inside out, so Sussex Street was to be avoided. The traffic had subsided only a few cars with glaring headlights getting the free wash from the rain. A pair of headlights flashed on the walls of the lobby and stopped our front. It had to be Sunny. I turned my collar up and made a charge for car gripping the brim of my hat.

The rear door opened as I reached it, so I only got a spray of rain for a few seconds before I slid into the backseat and slammed the storm out.

"Phew! What a night!" I said to Sunny behind the wheel. He just nodded. Not much for conversation we drove in silence through the storm and tempest to Roselle.

~ ~ ~

As we turned off Robert Street onto Port Access Road, I realized why the location had been selected: there were no street lights – warehouses and port facilities were all dormant this time of night – it was the archetypal set from some el cheapo Hong Kong gangster movie with the big shoot out at the end. I thought to myself *why is my job so full of fucking clichés?*

A few moments later the navigation aid told Sunny we were approaching 17A and he slowed the car.

Sunny spoke for the first time, "That's it on the right."

I was surprised by his voice it was half his size.

"Okay just pull up opposite."

I couldn't see a car parked anywhere. It was a complex of six warehouses that had seen their best years and then left deserted. Two old decrepit fishing trawlers were up on stilts at the waters edge and the only light came from the ambient glow of the city in the background across the bay.

The wind was being whipped up even stronger roaring across White Bay but at least the rain had quit.

"Are you carrying a piece?" I asked Sunny.

He leaned across to the glove compartment, opened it, and withdrew a Glock 37.

"Nice," I said. "Now listen, I'm going to check out those buildings over there for Jazz ... you keep an eye on me from the car, don't get out ... but if you see me in trouble or waving to you, don't hesitate to shoot whoever's giving me grief. You got that?"

His big head nodded.

"Okay, here we go," I growled revving myself up.

I stepped out into the misty rain and the dreadful gale hit me like a ton of bricks. Holding the brim of my hat I charged across the road, entered the property through an old gate swinging in the wind on rusted out hinges, and found cover under an awning. I couldn't be bothered playing hide and seek, so I called out at the top of my voice, "Jazz, its Axis, are you in there?" The roar of the wind was my only reply. There was a side door entrance to the first warehouse, I drew my pistol and made for it. I hate this sort of stuff. In the movies the music score makes a scene like this dramatic but in real life, screeching corrugated iron and stuff swinging in the gale is a score more creepy than dramatic. With the vision of Fatty stepping out from the shadows with gun aimed at me dominating my mind, I pulled open the door and entered the building. It's at a time like this a torch would come in handy. Each step I made on the wooden floor echoed in the empty building. There was no one there I could feel it. I had to ask myself, where would I have dumped Jazz? I'd put my money on the office building where there'd be more rooms to hide in ambush.

I slipped back outside and took in the wide-shot of the complex ... the building in the center, the only one with a front door had to be the old office. Just as I headed for it the skies opened up. It had a porch and I nearly slipped base over apex negotiating the four stairs up to it trying to avoid water gushing out of the rust eroded guttering. Back to the wall, I leaned forward to take a peek inside through the shattered window. It's the office all right – there was a reception at the front and a corridor leading to what I estimated to be about six offices. She wasn't in the front one, it was empty – but like before if it had been me, I would have put her deeper inside, to draw me in. Now it was going to get sticky.

I pushed open the door and with my .38 up, slipped inside and bellowed,

"Jazz, are you there? It's Axis."

From a lull in the rain beating on the iron roof, I heard a muffled but frantic groan further inside.

"I hear you Jazz, keep making a noise so I can find you."

Broken glass crunched under my boots, water streamed through holes in the busted ceiling and splashed on the floor, all that and the drumming of the rain made it difficult to hear her. I crossed the room ready to shoot anything that moved. It was dark and tough to find a clear path through all the fallen debris to where I figured she should be. Finally the rain eased off enough for me to get a good read on her. She was in the next office to the left of the corridor, but building materials were blocking the entrance. I kept on walking in a kind of blind man's shuffle – it was slow going. My head bumped into something solid which hurt, and my exploring fingers came up with the answer – it was part of the collapsed ceiling. Then Fatty made a mistake, he shuffled, and in that moment of calm, I heard the slightest sound of glass crunch under his shoes. He was in the office directly opposite Jazz, waiting, watching ... probably with a clear shot at me if I tried to enter through the only door to her. I had one advantage: it was just as tough for him to see me as it was for me to see him. I had to beat him at his own game. I removed my hat and coat ... got down on my hands and knees and crawled along the corridor on my belly like a snake. The rain started up again drumming on the roof and that covered me enough to move quicker. I made it past the entrance to the room he was in. As I got to my feet a lightning flash illuminated the corridor and for the first time I could see what I was up against. Right outside the door to Fatty's room on my side of the corridor was a wooden office desk smashed in half. If I could get behind it and get a bead on Fatty during a flash of lightning, I just might get a shot at him. He wouldn't be expecting me to shoot at him from there. Thunder rumbled. I worked out the lightning flashes were three minutes apart. The next one would be my signal to scoot to the broken desk and line him up for shot in the next flash. It was a roll of the dice that just had to be made.

The flash came, the rain drummed and I scurried to the desk ... I was lucky the ensuing thunderclap covered the clunk of me knocking the desk with my knee as I reached it. Ouch! It hurt. Shielded behind the desk, I aimed blindly into the dark at where I figured he was and counted down with my heart in my throat for the next flash of lightning.

It came right on time – I sighted him and fired – it was

over in the blink of an eye and I had no idea if I'd hit him or
not. I listened for the sound you'd expect to hear from
someone wounded – but heard nothing. There was no
alternative but to wait for the next flash. The thunder
resounded and the entire place shuddered. Jazz squawked.
I figured after hearing the gunshot she must be wondering,
which one of us was hit.

I took aim at the same spot ready for the next flash.

The flash came but there was no one there. He'd moved
– there had to be a back door to the room. It was my chance
to make a break to get to Jazz. I waited for the lightning to
guide me and when it flashed, I rushed in through the door
and found her tied and gagged in the corner of the room. It
was lucky she was in her underwear and it was white
otherwise it would have been difficult to find her in the
dark. Thunder sounded, more distant – the storm was
passing. I drew my flick-knife and cut her free of her bonds.
She stood up and hugged me.

"Oh Axis," she said tearfully.

"Come on, Tung is still on the loose."

I led her into the corridor, found my coat and put it
around her. I picked up my hat and then we rushed into the
front office.

"See the car, Sunny is there. You'll have to make a run
for it ... but lose the coat otherwise our friend might take a
pot shot at you thinking you're me."

"Okay, I can do it. What are you going to do?"

"I'm going to hunt down this bastard and blow a hole in
him."

"Why don't we just go?" she pleaded.

"Because he'll only come after me ... only one winner is

coming out of here tonight."

"Who is he?"

"Long story, he's Tung a Triad hit-man from Hong Kong, it seems I've offended him enough to warrant being whacked."

I walked her out onto the porch. I could see bloody footprints and realized the broken glass had lacerated her feet.

"You feet are cut, can you run?"

"I can't feel a thing ... are you on about feet again?"

"I can't help myself. Okay, when I say go drop the coat and run like the devil."

I waited until I felt the moment felt right and then said, "Okay, go!"

She slipped out of the coat and took off into the light rain running like a gazelle. She was a sight for sore eyes with her underwear now wet rendering it see-through.

The rear door of the car opened as she reached it and she disappeared safely inside. I put my coat and hat back on ready to hunt down the bastard.

CHAPTER
TWENTY-FIVE

A shot rang out and a bullet ricocheted off the building cornice missing my face by about six inches. It did something other than scare the living shit out of me: it gave away his position. With stealth I hugged the façade of the building with my back and crept along it to stop him from getting another shot at me. When I came to the last building I knew he had to be near to where he'd peeled off that last shot at me, so I figured he was just around the corner of the building. I heard the car window open and glanced in time to see Sunny's arm appear and aim the Glock in my direction. Immediately I knew what he was thinking. The Glock 37 forty-five caliber handgun not only packs a high velocity wallop but it's bloody loud. It has a ten round magazine. I counted off his shots, as he fired the seventh into the corner of the building just three feet from me, it was not only good grouping but it confirmed Fatty was there, Sunny could see him ... plus the salvo provided me cover to make a move. I waved my arm furiously at Sunny and took off at speed. Once clear of the corner of the building I dived onto the ground, paratrooper rolled on my left shoulder and came up on one knee with my .38 aimed at Fatty. He was on his knees no more than twenty feet from me, hugging the wall of the building.

"Drop it!" I ordered.

I could see he was hit by the way he was favoring his left arm, my shot earlier must have winged him. The seconds ticked away – he was holding his pistol up but not aimed at me. He knew if he tried to make a move I'd shoot ... and I wasn't going to miss at that range. He slowly lowered his gun hand in surrender and then struggled to his feet. I stood up with my gun trained on him. No way I was going to trust the bloke.

"Drop your gun now, Fatty!" I shouted.

"Fuck you!" he shouted and whipped his gun up to fire. I squeezed off a shot before him and blood, bone, hair and brain matter splattered on the faded yellow brick wall at back of him painting a gruesome but personal portrait. With a size .38 hole in his cheek just under his left eye and the back of his head gone, his legs crumbled and he hit the deck, dead meat. I holstered my weapon, dusted myself down, turned my back on the corpse and while walking to the car drew my phone and speed dialed Rick.

"Hey, yep, it's me ... I live again. Better send the meat wagon to 17A Port Access Road, Rozelle, got that? Yeah, they can tag the body bag Fatty Tung ... Yeah, I'll wait for them ... Yep, she's fine ... Okay, I'll bring her there in the morning. Thanks mate, Ciao."

When I climbed into the car I was surprised to find Jazz dressed. Sunny had thought to bring her a change of clothes.

"Much obliged, Sunny. Your cover shots did the trick."

He turned from the driver's seat and beamed me a big gold-toothed smile, "No worries, boss. It was Miss Sun's idea."

I called Ty and put Jazz on the phone to speak to her father in Chinese.

Ten minutes later I noticed the flashing lights of approaching cop cars: a meat wagon and a patrol car. When they stopped I got out, introduced myself and then walked them over to the corpse. One of them was forensics and she took photographs of the corpse, the spatter and the general crime scene. I was then required to recite an account of events into a hand recorder to be time stamped as evidence and then to hand over my pistol for ballistics. The cop then took a statement from Jazz and Sunny, and we were free to go.

Jazz cuddled up beside me with her head on my shoulder and we sat in silence on the back seat of the car all the way back to town. Ty had insisted on taking Jazz to the restaurant, so Sunny stopped us at the rear. We got out and Jazz led me through the kitchen to the private room. You would have expected a teary reception but no, it was as though Jazz had only been away for a weekend holiday. *Odd folk these Chinese*, I thought. By then it was after midnight, I'd downed a couple of JD's and was feeling pretty knackered, totally not in the mood for hearing Ty and Jazz babbling on in Chinese, for me her full account of the kidnapping could wait until tomorrow.

"Sorry to interrupt but I'm pretty stuffed so I'm going to bail and hit the hay," I said cutting into their conversation. "Jazz, you're required at police HQ at 9 a.m."

"That'll be fine. Want us to pick you up out front your apartment at 8.30?" she asked.

"Good–o, see you then, goodnight, Ty."

"Thank you Axis, and well done. I knew we could count

on you."

"It'll be in the bill," I joked.

As I walked through the empty restaurant I noticed Sunny sitting alone at a table eating.

I rested my hand on his big shoulder and said, "You did well tonight Sunny."

"No worries, boss," he smiled, and then went back to his congee, then looked up in an afterthought. "You want me to drive you home?"

"No thanks, mate. The walk will do me good."

~ ~ ~

It wasn't raining or windy outside. I looked up into the sky as the clouds parted to display a big full moon to beam down on me. I thought, *it's no wonder there were so many lunatics about tonight.*

There was a winter nip in the air that caused me to make the ten-minute walk to my apartment block in record time.

When I got inside I rang Nick.

"Hey, Nick. Yep, I made it but Fatty didn't."

"Jesus, Axis, are you okay? Tell me about it?"

"Fatty had taken control of the kidnapping and had Jazz at an old disused warehouse at White Bay docks. She was in a half demolished office in her underwear hogtied and gagged and Fatty was waiting for me."

"A trap?"

"You bet. Anyhow I managed to get a shot and winged him. He took off ... I got Jazz to the safety of the car and then went after Fatty. Ty's bodyguard Sunny was my driver and he hung out of the limo window with a Glock 37 giving me the cover to corner Fatty. I gave the guy a chance to surrender but he tried to take potshot at me and I hit him first."

"Dead?"

"As a doornail. He's on a slab in city morgue right now."

"Wow, mate, sounds like a close call. What's the next move?"

"Debriefing at police HQ with Rick and Parker in the morning. That's when we'll get the whole story from Jazz. They're holding Fang, so I expect they'll get Jazz to ID him and that might open him up, but somehow I doubt it."

"Yeah, I'm with you ... he won't risk it. His own gang will hunt him down and kill him if he blows the whistle on them."

"What's news at your end?"

"We're flying to Uluru tomorrow afternoon. Why don't you meet us there? Lola's coming as well ..."

"No, man, this case isn't over yet. We still have to sort out Grant Lee and who killed Rosy ... Besides, what's going to happen when the Dragon Head discovers that Fatty's dead and they only got a two hundred grand instead of two-mill?"

"I spoke to Ty earlier tonight. He rang me just to talk and he said he only sent fifty thousand."

"He's a sly bugger. That's the problem with him, just when you think you can trust the guy he does something like that and then keeps it from me ... reminds me of someone else."

"I thought you'd say that. I guess it's in our Chinese genes ... anyhow, you're damn right ... Lee Kok Lung isn't going to be impressed when he finds out. Might be a good idea to call Zhong tomorrow and tell him what happened to

Fatty, he'll be pleased ... plus he could alert immigration to keep an eye out in case Lee sends another hitman."

"I don't think he'll do that. More likely he'll get someone from here to take out Ty. He won't find out I killed Fatty. He'll think it was the cops and I'll see to it that's how it looks, that way I'll be clear of reprisals."

"Yes, that's sound thinking. All right mate, glad you're alive. You've done a top job again, my friend."

"Thanks, mate. Oh, by the way, I rang Suzie but I couldn't stop her blubbering long enough to get a word in."

"Yes, I've had reports she's been upset. You'll need to see her, Axis."

"Mate, the last thing I need now is women problems," I admitted.

"I thought you told me that was an occupational hazard," he said smugly.

"Goodbye, Nick. Have a good time at Uluru and say hi to the girls for me."

I hung up, poured myself a JD, kicked my boots off, and sat on the couch with my feet up on the coffee table. It was only ten-thirty in Hong Kong, so I decided to give Zhong a call.

"Hey, Zhong, it's Axis."

"Hello, Axis, how is it all going?"

"I just thought you should know that Fatty Tung is in Sydney morgue with bullet in his head."

"You've made my day, Axis," he said cheerfully. "Did the kidnapping turn out okay?"

"Yes, we got Jazz Sun back in one piece and now all we have to worry about is Lee Kok Lung's brother and any reprisals."

"What do you mean by reprisals?"

"Well, when Lee Kok Lung realizes he's been short changed and that his Red Pole is dead he might well react."

"No, you can rest assured nothing will come of it. He has lost two men on this deal, it wasn't worth it … he'll now leave it up to his brother to sort out."

"I'm happy to take your advice on that, mate. You have all the experience with these Triad dudes, I'm all at sea trying to understand them."

He chuckled. "Let me know if you need anything else, Axis," he assured me.

"Okay, Zhong. Take it easy, mate."

I put my phone on the coffee table, drained my glass of the last drip of JD, and then dragged myself off to the sack for a well-earned sleep.

~ ~ ~

The skies were clear and the morning sun streamed into The Grind Café. I'd just finished my morning coffee when the limo pulled up outside. I paid and headed out in time to find Sunny fending off a parking cop. We drove off before he could write a ticket. Poised on the back seat Jazz looked a picture of oriental delight, dressed in a red cheongsam split all the way up revealing a sexy naked leg. Her hair was held up in a bun by two black and gold lacquered chopsticks. Her bright red lipstick and matching fingernails almost completed the look until I noticed her red toenails protruding from her red Christian Louboutin T-Strap sandals.

"You look stunning today."

She looked over the top of her sunglasses at me. "Thank you, Axis. No suit for you?"

"No, my uniform is black jeans, INXS T, black leather jacket and sneakers."

"Hmm, macho," she said huskily and raised her eyebrows.

~ ~ ~

Sunny dropped us off out front of Police HQ and I led Jazz inside to the elevator.

On the way up she asked, "We haven't talked over what happened at all. Do I tell the truth or leave some out?"

"No need to leave anything out … just be upfront."

"What about the money transfer, have you told them how much Daddy actually sent?"

"Not yet. I only found out last night when I rang Nick. Your father hasn't been very forthcoming with important details like that."

CHAPTER
TWENTY-SIX

We got out of the elevator at homicide and walked through the open plan office towards Rick's private office at the back. Heads were turning at a terrific rate at Jazz strutting her stuff like a high fashion catwalk model.

Her look got me a wink and a sly grin from Rick when we entered his office but it seemed to leave Parker cold. I figured it was probably just a little feminine rivalry. After introductions we all sat down to listen to Jazz's account of the kidnapping from day one. Rick turned on a recorder ID'd and date stamped it for evidence, then signaled for Jazz to begin.

Her body language showed signs of being intimidated by the recording, but nevertheless wringing her hands, she proceeded like a trooper.

"I was in the bedroom when I heard a noise in the lounge room. Thinking it was probably just the guard getting a drink of water or something, I went to check. Three guys with stockings over their faces were tying the cop up. His face was all battered and bloody. I think he was unconscious. One of them had a knife. He spoke to me in Chinese, Cantonese with a thick southern accent. The other two stayed silent. I figured they were all armed, so I wasn't about to make a scene. The guy with the knife took hold of my arm and with the other two following behind, we went down in the elevator and out to a car that was illegally parked out front of the Connaught. Another guy was waiting in the car behind the wheel, he was the driver."

"Was he masked as well?" Rick asked.

"No, but I didn't have time to see his face because as soon as they got me onto the back seat they pulled a hood over my head. We went to Axis' apartment and then after that ..."

"Okay, is there anything you can think of that could help us identify any of these men?" Parker queried.

"No, they all stayed silent while we drove somewhere ... it felt like an hour with the hood on but it was probably only twenty-five minutes in reality. When we got to where ever it was the car went over a bumpy section, then stopped, someone got out and I heard a garage roller door open and then the car went inside. The garage door closed, they all got out except the guy next to me ... he tied my hands, legs and then gagged me. He left the hood on me, pushed me down on the seat and left me there. I heard a door open and close. That's where I stayed until last night."

"Did they feed you give you water?" Parker asked.

"Yes, at meal times the same guy returned with a bowl of rice and water. He would help me out of the car to have a pee."

"So he untied you?"

"No, he took the hood off, pulled down my panties and sat me on a drum with a plank across it. Then he watched me pee. When I finished, he pulled up my panties and put me back in the car. He left the hood off ... I could breathe better then."

"Was he always wearing a stocking over his head?" Parker asked.

"Yes."

"And wearing the same clothes?" Parker continued.

"No, different each day but only slightly."

"So we can assume this guy probably wasn't staying there?" Rick posed.

"Maybe he was living there ... or just had a change of gear," I suggested.

"I think you're right, he was living there, because sometimes I could smell scented soap on him, like he'd only just taken a shower," Jazz explained.

"Would you recognize this guy if you saw him again ... with a stocking over his head of course?" Parker asked.

"Maybe, but I can't say for certain," Jazz admitted.

"So you didn't overhear any conversation at all, you know, them talking on phones, chatting a distance away ... anything?" Rick probed.

"No nothing," she said dispiritedly.

Our body language had sunk with desperation, it appeared the kidnappers knew what they were doing and had covered their tracks professionally.

"There is one thing, but it's only small," Jazz said.

"Go on Jazz it doesn't matter how small," I said encouragingly.

"In the morning they gave me congee. It's a traditional Chinese breakfast that's like porridge only made from rice. Well, it was no ordinary congee ... it was jook, which is Cantonese congee and it takes a long time to cook."

"What are you saying Jazz?" Parker asked, wondering where she was going with the statement.

"Well, I doubt they could have cooked it at the premises, jook is difficult to make, it must have come from a nearby Chinese restaurant."

We exchange baffled looks then the penny dropped for me.

"Fortune Garden! They must have been near it."

"Well if they were at Alexandria where we triangulated Fang's call, they would only be ten, fifteen minutes away," Rick declared.

"Will that help?" Jazz asked.

"Just more ammunition to use on Fang Peng Jian we have in custody," Rick said.

"How much longer can you hold him Rick?" I questioned.

"Only till the end of today."

"So he's said nothing – not a word?" I challenged.

"Mate, he just sat there with a face like a slapped ass," Rick scoffed.

"Sir, I'd like to ask Miss Sun a couple more questions," Parker chimed in. Rick nodded affirmative and she continued, "Jazz, tell us about when they moved you last night?"

"Okay, I could tell there were only two of them and one of them was a new guy. He wasn't local, his clothes smelt of mothballs. They left me on the back seat tied and put the hood back over my head. They sat in the front. Someone opened the roller door and we drove out. We drove for about forty minutes in pouring rain. We went over a bridge, I could tell by the sound ... then shortly after that we stopped and the mothball guy dragged me out of the car ... he had calloused hands and was rough with me ... not like other guy before who had smooth hands ... there was lightning and thunder. He turned me around, took the hood off me, untied my hands and feet, and then took off my clothes and shoes, leaving me in my underwear. Then he put the hood back on me and retied my hands. The car drove off with my clothes and he grabbed my hand and led me inside a building. There was broken glass on the floor I could feel it cutting the soles of my feet. When I complained he just dragged me harder. I was wet and freezing. He stopped in a room, pushed me down onto the floor and then took off the hood so I could see."

"Did you see his face?" Parker asked.

"No it was too dark. But I could see he had a gun in his hand. After that Axis turned up."

"The hood was uncovered from the crime scene, sir and Fatty Tung's clothes did smell of mothballs," Parker concluded.

"Okay, thanks Jazz, all we need now from you is to identify the man we have in custody. Parker could you go down and prepare the suspects please?" He checked his wristwatch. "We'll be good to go in fifteen minutes."

"Yes sir." She got up and left.

"What are you thinking about Axis?" Rick asked aware I was pondering something.

"I'm just wondering how we can use the congee connection to Fortune Garden," I admitted.

"Jook, it's called jook," Jazz corrected me.

"That's it, let's tell Fang we're holding a cook from the Fortune Garden kitchen that we caught on CCTV delivering food to a warehouse in Alexandria."

"No mate, it wouldn't work ... look, the truth of it is if

Jazz can't ID him then we're sunk. We'll have to let him go."

"Fair enough. I figured it was probably a long shot," I accepted.

We sat around silently mulling over Jazz's story searching for clues until eventually Rick checked his watch and decided it was time to head down to the interview rooms.

"I'm a little nervous," Jazz admitted in the elevator. "Everything seems to be riding on me recognizing this guy."

"Calm down, kiddo. Either you'll know him or you won't. Just be honest," I said hoping to comfort her.

"We will also be studying him to see if he recognizes you. Parker is trained in doing that," Rick said.

That seemed to settle her nerves a little.

We left the elevator and Rick led us into a room and told us to take a seat. A few minutes later a uniformed police officer led six men into the room in single file ... it was an old fashioned line up, these days called an identity parade. Each was assembled under a number stenciled on the back wall. Parker entered by the same door and sat at the front close to the line up. The suspects were ordered to face directly in front – they were of similar height and stature and all Chinese.

"Take your time to study each face Jazz," Rick told her.

She nodded. After five minutes Parker stood and handed out a stocking to each man along with instructions to pull it over his head. They all complied. I had no idea which of them was Fang.

Jazz took her time deliberating but I could tell by the quizzical look on her face she was struggling.

After a while Parker nodded to the uniformed officer

and he marched the suspects out. Parker joined us.

"Well, what do you think?" Rick asked Jazz.

"I could have seen any one of them before at the Golden Dragon, but no, when they put the stocking on, the guy I caught only a short glimpse of certainly wasn't there."

"Are you certain, Jazz?" Parker almost pleaded.

"Positive," Jazz said emphatically.

Rick glanced at me with a raised eyebrow, "Fang was number five."

I sat with my elbows on my knees and my face in my hands. Rick was pacing the floor. Jazz was feeling like she'd spoilt the party.

Not wanting to appear defeated Parker questioned enthusiastically, "So, where do we go from here?"

I looked up from my hands and muttered, "For a mug of strong, freshly brewed coffee I reckon."

~ ~ ~

Fifteen minutes later we were sitting around a table in a quaint little café in Wentworth Avenue, just around the corner from Police HQ. Four coffees arrived and I think we were unanimous in the belief that the caffeine would fire up the necessary neurons for us to conjure up the next move.

"I don't know about you, but I'm fresh out of ideas," Rick admitted.

"Do you have a suspect for uncle Chiang's murder?" Jazz asked.

"No, nor the murder of Rosy Tong ... we have our suspicions but they won't give us an arrest," Rick conceded.

The melancholy had really set in when all of a sudden *Someday Soon* cranked up. It was Ty, to report someone had phoned him and threatened his life. It was just the break we needed, contact with the bad guys ... it meant the game was still in play but with a new threat: the stakes had increased. Ty was shaken. As a result he was holed up at his Darling Harbor apartment with two armed bodyguards for protection.

"What exactly was said, Ty?" I asked him as I put him on speaker.

"He said it wasn't enough money, that I had robbed him and he will feed me to the sharks like he did my brother if I don't pay up."

"Anything else?"

"He said everyone I know is in danger and he can wait, for a year, even more if he wants to ... he is in no hurry, the sooner I pay up then the safer everyone will be. It's a siege. Axis."

"Was that it?" I queried.

"No, he said for me to carefully consider my actions and he will be in touch. Oh, he had a Aussie Chinese accent, he spoke English."

"Okay, that's interesting. We'll be there within the hour."

"No hurry, I'm not going anywhere," he said disconsolately.

I pocketed my phone and stared at Rick. "Well, the beat goes on."

"Sure does, but it doesn't get any easier," he observed.

"So was he threatening Daddy and me?" Jazz mumbled.

"Yes, and anyone else associated with you," I added.

"So that means you," Jazz said to me.

TWENTY-SEVEN

"He's saying he means business, especially by stating he's prepared to wait Ty out," Parker submitted.

"Like Ty said ... a siege ... look if we agree that Grant Lee is behind this, and I'd say he was the caller - then we need to come up with a way of flushing him out into the open. He's all we've got," I proposed aggressively.

"You're right," Parker said. "When the hunter becomes the hunted."

"Waxing lyrical, Parker?" I mused.

"Not really. What I'm saying is we've been waiting for him to make a move and because of that we've been treating him as the hunter, now we need to hunt him ... turn the tables on him," she said with a spinning motion of her hands to demonstrate.

"So what do you have in mind?" Rick questioned.

"Well, like my dear old Dad used to say, *its the devil you know* ... so let's invite him into our ranks on the case and then wait for him to make a mistake," I posed.

It was an epiphany, a moment of divine inspiration and we reveled in it. Rick and Parker raced back to HQ to put the wheels in motion, while Jazz and I went searching for Sunny to take us to Ty's apartment.

~ ~ ~

If the Connaught apartment Jazz owned was the Ritz

then Ty's penthouse apartment on the sixty-first floor of World Tower by comparison was Buckingham Palace. When we entered, I was immediately struck by the one hundred and eighty degree spectacular view of Sydney - it was nothing short of mind-boggling. Darling Harbor on one side, Sydney Harbor, the Opera House and the Harbor Bridge on the other, and lounging back on a huge black leather lounge dressed in a robe and looking like King Farouk was Ty.

"Come in, come in ... sit down, Axis. Jazz, get him a drink, there's a good lass," he crowed.

Jazz didn't look impressed by the command but obliged anyway. Sunny joined the other two bodyguards on the balcony.

"Nice chunk of real estate, Ty," I said looking around.

"It's convenient," he said a little cockily. It was to be expected.

"So our problem didn't leave us with the death of the Red Pole, did it?" he said dispiritedly.

"What do you expect after paying only fifty-grand," I said with a modicum of scorn.

I watched Jazz go to the bar. It was equipped to handle a three-day convention of alcoholics. She carried two glasses back, handed me one and then sat in an armchair facing me. I could smell it was JD.

"Cheers to beating the bad guys," I said raising my glass.

"I don't suppose the police have any ideas, do they?" Ty asked stiffly.

"More than you expect, Ty, after all they still have two unsolved murders on their hands."

"So what are they going to do about this threat? I don't want to be imprisoned in my own home," he growled bitterly.

"If you had paid the correct amount you probably wouldn't be having this problem, Ty," I snapped back.

He stood up, fuming.

"I don't pay you to chastise me, Stone!" he shouted savagely.

"You pay me for my advice and you put everyone at risk by short paying the ransom without telling me. I put my life on the line for you, old fella, and I expect the respect to be told the truth. Now sit down, you're displaying your anger like a peacock on heat and it means fucking nothing to me. If you want help then get rid of the attitude, otherwise pay me out and I walk," I growled harshly.

He fired me a dark glare and then sat back down on the lounge brooding.

"He's right, father. He's all you've got so I'd be treating him with respect if I was you, he saved my life, did he not?"

Ty seemed to take Jazz's statement on board and calmed down.

"Please accept my apology, Axis. I'm out of line, I should have told you about the payment. Please stay on the case, we need you."

"Okay, apology accepted. Look, Ty, I don't know any better alternative to you staying holed up here for the next few days. We need to give the cops a chance to flush the villain out … you're safe here. Can Jazz stay here as well?"

"I'd rather not," she said crisply.

"I'll put some bodyguards on her as well. Sunny will take care of that," Ty said.

"You'll have to stay in your apartment then, Jazz," I added.

"I can handle that," she agreed.

"Who else is there in your family?" I asked.

"Only Sherri, my uncle's daughter. She's the same age as me and lives in Rockdale."

"Is she married? Does she work?" I queried.

Ty and Jazz shared a sheepish glance.

"She isn't married ... she owns and operates a massage parlor in Rockdale. We have nothing to do with her," Ty muttered dispassionately.

I thought *oh no, here we go again with his prejudice.*

"Would she know her father is dead?" I pressed.

"We wouldn't know," Ty said dismissively.

"Okay, give me her contact details. I'll go and see her today,"

"Why?" Jazz asked.

"Because I think she would be next on the list to hit," I said assertively. "He'll take out the easiest to get to demonstrate his superiority, and she'd be it for sure."

"You've got to be kidding. Just phone her and tell her. There's no need for you to go to any trouble," Ty said.

"You don't seem to be taking the threat very seriously when it comes to other people Ty," I criticized him.

"She's good for nothing, Axis, not worth the trouble."

"Let me be the judge of that," I said in a hard voice. "Remember Rosy?" I reminded him.

"She doesn't pay your fee, I do, and I say she's not worth the trouble," Ty said emphatically.

"Think about this, Ty, she might just represent our best chance of catching this bastard," I eyeballed him.

Though his lack of humanity was abhorrent even he could see the logic in my suggestion.

"So will you use her as bait?" Ty asked with a smirk.

"I guess you could call it that."

~ ~ ~

I took a cab to 93A, Railway Street, Rockdale. A dinky little shop with a sign out front that read Magic Hands Massage. The front window and door were covered in Chinese symbols. I opened the door and a bell rang ... I was immediately overcome by a powerful waft of jasmine.

A stunning looking Chinese woman appeared from behind a curtain, smiled warmly and then said in broken English, "Hello sir, you come for massage, I give very good hand job with half hour massage, just seventy dollar."

"Are you Sherri Sun?"

"Yes," she said and wrinkled her brow.

"I'm Axis Stone, a private detective. Can we talk somewhere private?"

"Yes, come in to my parlor," she said dropping the phony broken English.

I was led into a massage room and sat on the edge of the massage table while she sat in a chair and crossed her long bare legs. I glanced at her sandaled feet. It seemed that beautiful petite feet ran in the Sun family. If ever I needed a massage I'd sure be calling on Sherri.

"What do you want to ask me? I hope I haven't offended some gentleman's wife," she said with a sexy wry smile.

"No, It's nothing like that ... I'm working for your uncle Ty Sun."

Her expression soured.

"Is this about my father?"

"Yes, in part."

"I already know he is dead; the police contacted me."

"I'm sorry, Miss Sun."

"Don't be. We are an estranged family ... dysfunctional I suppose you'd call it. Ty and his daughter don't approve of me or my business."

"Miss Sun ..."

"Please, call me Sherri."

"The people who murdered your father have threatened the lives of all the Sun family, which includes you. That is what I'm here to tell you."

"So, for the crimes of my family, who frown on what I do, my life is being threatened. That's a little ironic don't you think?" she said with a cute smile.

"Yes, I'd have to agree with you."

"Pathetic, so, what do you want me to do, Axis?"

"I want you to help me catch the gangsters that murdered your father and his girlfriend."

"Oh, they killed Rosy as well? She was a good kid, worked here for twelve months until her family found out and told Ty. He took her away to be his and turned her into my father's concubine. I think she was better off giving hand jobs with a massage, with no strings attached ... at least she'd still be alive if she'd stayed here. I am sorry to hear she's dead."

"You make sense, Sherri. So what do you say ... will you help?"

"I'll do it for Rosy."

"Thank you, I knew her as well. She was a lovely girl."

"So what do you want from me, to use me to lure a man?" She grinned amorously. "I'm good at that."

"Can you come with me now to meet the police on the case?"

"This is my business, and like my legs, I can open and close when I like. Just give me a minute to change." She stopped at the door. "You sure you don't want a massage first?"

"Not tonight, honey," I said sadly.

After a sexy wink she disappeared behind a curtain.

"I suppose Ty and Jazz have locked themselves in their apartments with armed guards," she called out from somewhere out back.

"You've got it."

"The police told me I should inherit my father's apartment but apparently Ty thinks it is his."

"Will you contest it?"

"Unfortunately for Ty, I'm in my father's will. I just don't know if I want to live there."

The curtain opened and an even more stunning woman glided back into the room. She was dressed in a silver cheongsam split up to the hip exposing a pair of magnificent bare legs. Around her shoulders she wore a long, light gray cashmere shawl. Her hair was up, which showed off her lovely, long, taped neck.

"I am ready. Shall we go then?" she beamed.

I took her by the arm and walked her out to catch a taxi to Police HQ.

~ ~ ~

In the cab on the way I wondered what are all the cops at homicide were going to think of me this time with Sherri hanging off my arm? I could hardly wait to see the look on Parker's face.

Just as we were getting out of the taxi *Someday Soon* started up. It was Nick.

"Hey, Nick, how's Uluru?"

"We didn't make it there. Kitty's birthstone is opal, so she wanted to go to Winton for me to buy her one - there are opal mine here. So I rented a plane and that's where we are."

"A bit off the beaten track, isn't it?"

"Not really. It's Central West Queensland, so I suppose it's on the way to Uluru. Anyhow, Ty called me and asked me to come to Sydney to help protect him, I thought I'd better ring you first."

"The guy's a drama queen when it's about him. I don't think there's anything you can do, just enjoy your holiday with Kitty."

"And Lola."

"Oh, right."

"I wanted to tell you we were in the bar of the Australian Hotel last night and met a bloke from Sydney. He's an opal dealer and a composer. A good bloke, he's going to write a song for Kitty to sing."

"Cool."

"His name is Rod and he's got a brother who is an author and has a problem that needs a private eye. Do you want me to recommend you?"

"Sure, tell him I don't do divorce spying ... and it will have to wait until this case is over. Thanks."

"No problem. You'll have a lot in common. He lived in Manila for ten years or so and owned a third share in Foxy's girlie bar. That was the club Ringo Raye owned, wasn't it?"

"Sure was. He probably knew him," I confirmed.

"Anything new on the case?" he enquired.

"I've got Sherri Sun with me right now on our way to meet with Malone and Parker."

"Sherri? Chiang's daughter?"

"Yes."

"The black sheep of the family," he chuckled.

"I'd be more inclined to say she's the white sheep and the rest of the family are the black one's."

"I hear you. Say hi to her for me. I haven't seen her since she was a little girl. I'll call you in a day or two."

"Okay, ciao," I turned to Sherri who was sitting on the low brick fence out front of Police HQ. "That was Nick Vargas. He asked to be remembered to you."

"Oh yeah, the Filipino leg of the family. He's an alright guy."

We went inside and caught a waiting elevator up to homicide.

CHAPTER
TWENTY-EIGHT

I was right about the reaction to Sherri; if Jazz turned heads then Sherri just about had them screwed off. Through the glass-paneled door I could see Rick and Parker making notes on the murder-board. I knocked on the door and then opened it.

"Rick, got a moment?"

"Come in, mate. Who's this?" he exploded with his eyes bugging out.

Parker turned from the board and reacted in a similar fashion, not at all the same as she had for Jazz. I suppose because Sherri wasn't reeking arrogance like Jazz had.

"This is Sherri Sun, daughter of Chiang Sun, and she's here to help us," I announced.

The discussions went well, and within an hour we'd hatched a plan to expose the killer. But it meant me staying at Sherri's house in Rockdale.

DS Grant Lee would be brought into the case tomorrow under the guise that Rick needed an investigator on board with special knowledge of Triads and fluent in Cantonese. There would be no mention of the death threat against Sun family members. He would be told that I no longer had anything to do with the case, and that it was now a police investigation into the murders of Chiang Sun and Rosy

Tong. The bait was set in the trap now all we needed was for him to spring it.

I phoned Ty and Jazz, told them the plan and they bought into it. By sundown after picking up a few things from my apartment, Sherri and I were in a taxi on our way to her place at Kent Street, Rockdale.

~ ~ ~

It was a cul-de-sac with her house right at the end. An old Federation red brick house that from the outside didn't look her speed at all. The taxi pulled up in the driveway and we got out.

"I only rent it but it suits me fine. I live alone and like the walk to work from here, everything I need is nearby," she said leading me up the fifteen red steps to the front door.

"You got a car?" I said looking at the red roller door on the garage.

"No, don't need one." We went inside. "There are three bedrooms, mine is the main take your pick from the other two."

"What's at the back?"

"A small backyard."

"Show me."

"Oh, I forgot you've got to do the James Bond thing and check the house out for when the crooks arrive," she said. I followed her down a hallway to the kitchen and the back door, checked the lock, and opened a small door off to the right.

"The laundry," she said smugly with her arms folded.

"Yes, with a window that's open," I said locking it. "I'll take the bedroom at the front of the house, so I can keep

240

an eye on things."

"But that's my bedroom," she complained.

"Bad luck," I said with a big Cheshire cat grin.

A couple of hours later I was sitting on the double bed reading when Sherri called out from the dining room.

"Dinner!"

She'd put on quite a spread with a number of small dishes in traditional Chinese fashion.

"Seems all I've eaten of late is Chinese food."

"Oh, of course you've probably been spoilt to death by all the lovely food at the Golden Dragon."

"Yes, plus I was in Hong Kong with Nick for a few days and he took me to a couple of his favorite haunts there."

"Great, how long have you known Nick?"

"I worked with him on a kidnapping case in Manila a few months ago, so not that long, but when you're put in life threatening situations with someone, it's amazing how you bond, it's now like we've been mates for years."

"That makes plenty of sense, he's a really rich guy but he remains humble, and that is the sign of a gracious person."

"Yes, he's very generous and caring ... that's rare as well, rich or not."

"You're an oddball, Axis Stone," she smiled.

"Yeah, why is that, Sherri Sun?"

"You have a hardball job, you don't need to care about people but you do. It must be tough being a romantic in your game."

I sat back in my chair and looked her over. "I could say the same of you, couldn't I?"

"No, not at all, my lot in life is to give pleasure and I

pride myself in doing that."

"So giving pleasure gives you pleasure?"

"Yes, it's a Zen thing."

"Ah, so you're a Buddhist?"

"Sort of ... Tantric Buddhism or Vajrayana, and the study of Tantric sex."

"Tantric sex ... is that a style or a religion?"

"Tantric texts state that sexual activity can have three separate and distinct purposes: procreation, pleasure and liberation. Those who use tantric sex to seek liberation abstain from reaching an orgasm in favor of a higher form of ecstasy."

"And you practice that and teach it?"

"Yes."

"Where do I sign up?" I said with a chuckle.

She reached out, took my hand and gave it a gentle squeeze.

"Come." She walked me into the lounge room. It reminded me of a Hippy flat I been in once. I sat on the lounge that was draped in an Indian rug with elephants and tassels on it and she lit a stick of incense. She sat beside me and took my hand again. Then we were looking steadily into each other's eyes, and with my breath quickening, I knew we were on the brink of something. The air in the room was crackling with expectancy. She let go of my hand and rose to her feet.

"Can I get you a drink?" she said, moving over to a small bar.

"Yes, a neat bourbon if you have any."

"I do."

I leaned back on the sofa and watched the lithe, almost

athletic movement of her buttocks beneath the grey satin cheongsam she was wearing. I watched the dark Chinese dragons in the pattern of her dress appear to move with her. She poured me a drink and brought it back. Her small but ample breasts quivered beneath the dress.

"I enjoy being a happy person and making other people happy," she said, "in the terms of being fulfilled." She was looking into my eyes again, and it seemed the most natural thing in the world to slip my arm around her shoulder and ease her in to snuggle against me. She sighed. "That's nice, you have strong arms, Axis."

"All the better to hold you with," I countered.

I had moved my hand down and closed it over one breast, which I was gently squeezing. The firm flesh shifted beneath the pressure of my hand. I could feel her erect nipple against my palm.

"Do you have a lot of sex, Axis?"

"I take what I can get, I guess."

She turned her body against me, her lips seeking mine as her hand inched down to my hardening cock. We kissed warm and soft our tongues seeking a world of their own. Her fingers pressed my firm rod. My own hands caressed her breasts, which I had uncovered by unbuttoning the front of her dress and peeling it back off her shoulders.

Our movements quickened, became frantic. Her fingers fiddled with the zip of my jeans, then when she had it open, delved into the opening. The touch of her fingers on my hot flesh was cool. Her lips pulled away from mine. She slipped off the sofa onto the floor then moved in between my legs. She lowered her head and her moist lips gently closed around the tip of Mr. Happy, and then she drew it deep into her warm mouth.

It went on for some time like that, working on each other, building up the pitch until we were so close to orgasm and then she would ease back to then build the tension again. Our clothes were soon scattered on the floor. I rolled her on her back ... it was time to enter her. Her body writhed against mine and she arched her back to take me. I slid Mr. Happy inside her and felt the muscles of her sheath grip me like I've never felt before. She rolled me over and rode me at her pace – it was blissfully tortuous, my cock swelling wanting me to cum but she was in control easing off when she felt I was about to spill the soup.

She leaned forward and whispered huskily in my ear, "The ecstasy is in resisting the orgasm." She was panting with a hot breath and her face was flushed. She was riding me skillfully, her head back, her teeth bared and her naked body covered by a light sheen of perspiration. Her vaginal lips pulsed around my straining cock, holding it in place, reluctant to let it go as she moved up and down its length.

"Okay, are you ready?" she panted after the longest time I've ever lasted before ejaculating.

I nodded ... I couldn't speak.

Then she gave a sharp, shuddering cry and her body went rigid. Every muscle was tensed. Then her labial lips began to quiver ... I've not felt anything like it before ... then came a warm rush of her love fluid. I couldn't hold back any longer with a great surge I shot my seed – again and again until my balls ached and felt like prunes. We trembled and gripped each other tight to ride the wave after wave of her multiple orgasms, until she flopped onto my chest spent.

"I thought you weren't meant to cum?" I whispered

panting.

"Not this time," she groaned pleasurably and then cuddled up to me tighter.

~ ~ ~

It was in the small hours of the morning that I was suddenly awakened. I'd noticed when Sherri led me to bed, that the wooden floorboards creaked in certain places in the hallway, and that must have been in the back of my mind because a loud creak woke me. My .38 was in a carry bag beside the bed. I sat up sharply and reached down for it. Sherri was still sound asleep. I slipped out of bed, buck-naked, gun in hand, went to the bedroom door and stood so I'd be behind it when it opened. The door handle rattled ever so slightly, I held my breath and locked my finger on the trigger of the .38. The hinges squeaked as the door slowly opened. It wasn't too dark – enough of the streetlight outside streaming in through the bay windows allowed me to make out a guy dressed in black entering with what looked like a meat cleaver clutched in his hand. *Is there only one of them? Should I shoot him or just hold him up? Could I fight him naked?* Too many thoughts were spinning through my mind ... Instinct drove me, I lashed out and struck the hand carrying the cleaver hard with my pistol. It hit the floor with a loud clunk and woke Sherri. She sat up, gasped and turned on the bedside light. He was well in through the door so I threw a punch at his head. He anticipated it, ducked back and quickly pulled the door half closed in one sharp movement. My fist belted into the edge of the door and the pain shot up my arm like a lightning bolt. It felt like I had broken my wrist. Ignoring the pain, I quickly pulled the door open with my foot, and with the .38

held up to shoot, went after him. I heard movement in the hallway ... he was headed for the front door. It was darker there and all in black, he was just a fleeting shadow. I thought of peeling off a blind shot but decided against it. Suddenly, I saw light: he'd opened the front door to slip out. I ran after him outside onto the landing. He was too quick for me to get a bead on him. With the .38 aimed at him I watched along the sights as he disappeared inside a waiting car. It was already facing out of the cul-de-sac with the engine running and shot off. It had no plates. I charged down the stairs but by the time I got to the bottom it had gone.

The lights came on in the house opposite and an old lady ripped opened the curtains in the front room and gawked at me in wide-eyed terror. I suddenly realized I was standing stark naked with my .38 in my hand – no wonder she was all goggle-eyed.

CHAPTER
TWENTY-NINE

When I told Rick the story over the phone next morning, he found the tag most amusing but at the same time he was pissed the bastards had got away. This meant a change of plan because now they were aware Sherri was under protection. With my apartment a more secure option it was a no-brainer for Sherri to stay there and it didn't take much convincing. She packed some things and we took a cab to Regal Apartments.

On the way I phoned Jazz who wasn't impressed with Sherri moving in with me.

"Next you'll be sleeping with her, I know her she's a nympho and won't be able to keep her hands off you."

"Oh, I wouldn't be too worried about that Jazz, I can handle it," I scoffed, enjoying her jealousy.

"I'm sure you can. Anyway you're lucky you didn't get hurt in the attack."

"I'm going to the hospital after I drop Sherri off to get my wrist X-rayed, it's swollen up like a balloon and giving me buggery."

I got no sympathy from her. That was something she had in common with her father.

"So what's Rick's take on the next move?" She asked curtly.

"He and Parker are still mulling it all over."

In reality they had a meeting set with Grant Lee, but now the substance of the meeting as far a Sherri was concerned, had changed.

"Parker didn't like me did she?"

"I think she might have given that impression, but it's just her way of scrutinizing people, " I said dismissively, not interested to go there. "I'm going to ring Ty now, have you spoken to him today?"

"No. Okay, catch you later," she said abruptly and hung up.

I shrugged my shoulders and rang Ty. After giving him the same story as Jazz, I got the same reaction – he didn't give a shit about anything to do with Sherri, but was disturbed that the killer might now focus on him and Jazz.

"Listen, I checked my account today and you haven't paid me, can you fix that up today?" I grated.

"I'll fix it up when I'm convinced there's a plan," he stuttered frantically.

"Ty you're paying me for work done, I don't go risking my life for nothing, you owe me money so pay up or you'll find yourself working alone."

He got the hint and changed his tone.

"All right Axis, I'm sorry, I will deposit the money in your account today."

"Okay, I'll ring you back later with the new strategy."

I hung up thinking he wasn't going to pay me until he'd heard what he wanted to hear: that the coast was clear.

~ ~ ~

The coffee was brewing while Sherri cleaned up my apartment. There was quite a collection of dirty dishes and clothes to be washed.

I sat on the lounge with my coffee after lacing it with JD. Sherri came up behind me and massaged my neck, head and shoulders. That really got the blood flowing to my brain and started me thinking clearer.

"Your wrist looks like it might be fractured."

"Yeah, I'll go to St. Vincent's Hospital and get it X-rayed later this morning. It's bloody sore."

"They'll only set it and put it in plaster, do you want me to do it?"

"Why not, what do you need?

"These days you don't really need a plaster cast, we can get a fiberglass brace from a drug store."

"Okay, there's one in Chinatown, I'll check there."

"We'll need to get the swelling down first."

"That something you might not be good at, I think you're better at making things swell up, aren't you?" I said cheekily.

She poked me playfully in the shoulder.

Though my wrist was throbbing, I was still feeling pretty good about myself as I strode along Sussex Street on my way to the Chinatown pharmacy. It was a sunny day and good weather always perks me up. I was thinking about Nick and the fresh case he had for me. He'd sent me the contact for the author who needed a PI. It was good to know I might have another job after this one. Ty and Jazz were beginning to get up my nose, so the sooner this one was over the better. Suddenly, I thought of Suzie and decided to give her a quick call in Manila. It came as a surprise when the maid answered and told me Suzie had left. There was a note Dom had photographed and sent Nick. I hung up and immediately rang Nick but it went to his message bank, I told him to ring me.

For some reason while I was walking I recalled the nightmare of Rosy with the vampire teeth and all and wondered why it was still in my mind? I brushed the thought and entered the drug store only to reemerge ten minutes later with a carry bag containing a fiberglass wrist brace. The chemist had taken a look at injury and felt the joint, his diagnosis was that perhaps I had a slight fracture but more likely it was just a bad strain with deep bruising. He said the brace would do the job for the injury either way. Being Chinese, he decided it would be best for me to use White Flower Oil to hasten the healing and reduce the pain. So I bought a bottle as well seeing I was currently into all things Chinese.

It was only late morning I was expecting calls from Rick and Nick, so I called by the office on the way back to check my mail.

The post box was full of bills, brochures and pamphlets. There were so many letters of demand from my telco, I was surprised my phone hadn't been disconnected.

I discarded most of the crap in the bin and got into elevator. Just as I came out on my floor my phone rang. It was Nick.

"Hey Nick."

"We just got to Uluru."

"Look, I won't hold you up ... just wondering if you got a message from Dom about Suzie?"

"Yes, I was going to send it, we've only just landed."

"What does it say?" I said opening the door to my office and entering.

"She met a Taiwanese businessman at a shopping mall and she's gone to stay with him."

I flopped into the chair behind my desk and booted up my computer.

"Oh well *comme ci comme ça* – such is life," I said, nonchalantly.

"You're very prophetic today Axis."

"Yeah, it's either the busted wrist or the wonder of Sherri Sun."

"Oh no, you haven't have you?"

"Well, I don't have Suzie any more ... so ..."

"Axis, you can't control yourself. You need to see a therapist."

"Last time I saw a therapist I ended up having sex with her. No, I'm fine mate, it's just the way I am."

"Do you ever not have sex with your clients?"

"I've had a couple of granny's that I left to nature. Mate, a man has to back himself."

"You're despicable."

"So what now you're Daffy Duck, get out of here," I said jokingly. "Enjoy Uluru, and see if you can pick up a pair of Kurdaitcha shoes for me."

"What are they?"

"Aboriginals reckon when you're wearing them you become invisible."

"You'd only get into more trouble being the invisible man! See you Axis."

I chuckled to myself, Nick must think I'm a stud – hmm, maybe I am.

I wrote down the name and contact details of the guy Nick recommended me to for my next case and then attended to paying a bunch of outstanding bills on-line – at least my credit card was still functioning.

The pile up of e-mail went back to before the case started. It was totally unreasonable and took ages to download all two thousand of them. Most of them were spam, so I got into trashing them at a great rate. Suddenly I trashed one that rang a bell in a delayed reaction. I went back to the trash bin to look for it and found it was from rosyT177. I wondered if that was Rosy and it was – it said, *Last night was the best ever, love Rosy.* There was an attachment. When I opened it I nearly fell off the perch. She had e-mailed me before she was murdered – and it was what she said in her cryptic text message that I hadn't yet had time to decipher ... She said: *I sent you* ... and that's also what the vampire version of her told me in that bloody nightmare ... *I sent you* ... and she had. I turned on the printer.

Next, I phoned Rick. He was just about to start the meeting with Parker and Lee. So I had to leave a message for him to hang fire: I had something important and that I was on my way.

It didn't take me long to grab a cab out front of the office. I hopped in and immediately phoned Sherri to meet me right away out front the apartment block.

The cab pulled up just as she came out of the front doors.

~ ~ ~

Ten minutes later we stepped out of the elevator on the homicide floor of Police HQ. Sherri wasn't dressed to kill this time but she still managed to turn a few heads. I'd briefed her in the taxi as to what was about to happen in

Rick's office.

I knocked on the glass door.

"Come in, Axis," Rick called from inside.

We entered and sat in the chairs waiting for us.

"I think you'd better record this, Rick," I advised.

Parker got up, set up a microphone and then date and time stamped it on the computer.

"Recording," she confirmed.

Lee didn't look very comfortable with it being recorded but before he could protest I said, "Grant Lee, this is Sherri Sun, but then you already know that don't you?"

With furrowed brow he gave Sherri the once over. "No, I don't think I've ever had the pleasure. Why is this being recorded?"

I ignored his question, "Oh, but you knew her father Chiang Sun didn't you?"

"No, only by reputation," he said poker-faced.

I glanced surreptitiously at Rick and he gave me a nod to continue.

"When did you complete your last undercover assignment Detective Lee?" I asked sternly.

"August last year, that has nothing to do with this case? Rick, why am I being questioned, Stone isn't a police officer?" he complained, and was beginning to look a little unraveled.

"What is your Chinese name?" Parker continued.

"Lee Kit Wo. I still don't see the point of this," he growled intolerantly.

"What is your brother's Chinese name?"

"Lee Kok Lung."

Parker was taking notes while questioning. "Is your

brother Lee Kok Lung, the Hong Kong Dragon Head of the Triad movement Sun Yee On?" Parker asked stiffly.

"Yes, but it is a legitimate business," he said defensively.

"Do you know Fatty Tung?" I asked.

He jumped up out of his chair and snapped, "I'm not going to be subjected to questions from this man!"

"Sit down Detective Lee," Rick snarled. "I invited Axis Stone to this meeting to provide evidence in the shark leg case, you will answer his questions."

He slowly sat back down scowling.

"Do you know Fatty Tung?" I repeated.

"Yes, he works for my brother," he snarled indignantly. Why was he in Sydney this week?"

"I expect for business," he shrugged his shoulders.

"I put it to you that you are the Dragon Head of the Sydney chapter of Sun Yee On," Parker pressed him.

"That's absurd. In case you haven't noticed I'm a police officer," he said scornfully.

It was time to use my trump card. I pulled out two sheets of paper from my inside jacket pocket and unfurled them slowly. I watched Lee's beady eyes follow me as I stood and took a couple of steps to hand one to Rick. I turned slowly and handed the other to Lee and then sat back down.

Both men studied the page in their hands.

"Do you recognize the men in that photo detective Lee?"

"Yes, Chiang Sun, and myself" he said undaunted.

"Do you see the date on the photo detective Lee?"

He nodded and looked back at me smugly. His whole demeanor had changed, now he looked like a cheap gangster.

"You're on record as saying you never met Chiang Sun detective. Your undercover assignment finished in August last year, so what were you doing two months ago handing over drugs to Chiang Sun?" Parker barked.

"I might have been mistaken," he said calmly – nastily.

Sherri eyeballed him with a wicked glint in her eyes. Suddenly she jumped up and exploded at him, "You killed my father and you killed Rosy you bastard – murderer!" Then she launched a second tirade at him in Chinese. I used to think Cantonese sounded angry in normal conversation, but her attack was so venomous it made normal Chinese conversation seem submissive. Sherri had blown her top and she struck out at him with her long fingernails trying to claw his face off. Parker acted fast and managed to subdue her before she could do any damage. Rick nodded sharply towards the door for Parker to take Sherri outside.

"Lee Kit Wo, I'm charging you with the murder of Chiang Sun and the murder of Rosy Tong. I am also charging you with conspiracy to kidnap Jazz Sun," Rick announced emphatically.

A quick wave of his hand and two uniforms stormed into the office and cuffed Lee.

"Even your lousy photo won't be enough to make any of that stick Malone, you know that," he sniggered wickedly.

"If the photo isn't so damning then why did you kill Rosy for it?" I snarled.

I wanted to belt his supercilious head in, but I'd have to leave that for his cellmates.

I stood up and eyeballed him. "You're just a piece of shit Lee, you and your insignificant mob of thugs. This isn't China and your stand over tactics don't work here."

"We'll see about that," he cracked back at me through narrowed eyes.

"You've put shame on the trust given you as a police officer. By the time you get out of prison you'll be an old man full of regrets, so let's see about that!" I growled.

"Take him away," Rick roared dismissively.

As they took him out I noticed Sherri and Parker on their way back to the office. Sherri stopped in her tracks, fired Lee a wicked glare – if looks could kill. Then she shouted something at him in Cantonese.

"Sit down, Axis. A job well done, mate," Rick said. "How did you get the photo?"

"Rosy had e-mailed it to me before she was killed. I feel a complete idiot. It'd been there all along."

"You weren't meant to know she'd sent it."

"She sent a text with the words 'sent it' ... I had no idea what she meant. I only checked my e-mail today first time since I starting this case."

"Well, we'll be able to throw the book at him; the photo should make it stick," Parker said, sitting down.

"Maybe it'll help us crack Fang ... He might spill the beans once he knows we've got the Dragon Head," Rick added.

"I think you should have someone interrogate him in Chinese Detective," Sherri pointed out.

"I think she's right, it wouldn't hurt to fly Shun Zhong down from Hong Kong to do it, there's no one more savvy on Triads than him," I proposed.

"That's a great ideas Axis. I'll do that," Rick said.

"What did you screech at him in Cantonese, Sherri?" I asked.

"I told him I've come across some big dicks in my time but he is by far the biggest," she grinned cheekily.

Only I really understood her meaning.

Rick let it go over his head and said, "So, what's the next case, Axis?"

I raised my arm to show the wrist-brace. "Got to mend this first, then I'll see what washes my way." I got up. "Come on Sherri, let's go visit your relatives. See you later Rick … you too, Parker."

When we got outside I phoned Ty. He was over the moon when I told him the case was solved and he laid on the praise. I thought it ironic that Rosy, the girl he so maligned, was in the end his savior … but I didn't mention it for obvious reasons.

"Have you made the deposit in my account, Ty?"

"I was onto it when you called. Don't worry, you will be paid in full today."

I knew he was lying about being *onto it*, but I was confident he'd pay up now he had the good news.

"I'll give Jazz a call and tell her, keep the high security up till tomorrow, by then Rick will have lodged formal charges against Lee and the threat to both of you will be derailed."

"Thank you. Axis."

I hung up dialed Jazz and gave her the news. She got the irony of it and was thankful for Rosy's clever deed.

"Should I dismiss the bodyguard?" she asked.

"No, not until I give you the word. You're not safe until Lee is behind bars."

"Are you thinking there might be more reprisals for my father's actions?"

"How long is a piece of string? I can't answer that, honey. Right now we believe we have the Dragon Head of the Sydney chapter of Sun Yee On, who might well have been doing things on an agenda of his own ... or the whole issue was the machination of Lee Kok Lung, Dragon Head in Hong Kong and Lee was only a pawn in a much bigger game. In my book, the problem of why Fatty Tung came here for your handover has me baffled. Was it just to get square with me?" I posed.

"I see what you're saying. There could be a bigger picture," Jazz said a little nervously.

"We'll know when Rick and Parker get Lee to talk."

"And what are the chances of that?"

"Rick is going to fly Shun Zhong the boss of the Organized Crime and Triad Bureau in Hong Kong down here to interrogate him and Fang in Chinese, if anyone can do it I'd put my money on Zhong."

"That's an excellent idea. Look, how about coming over for dinner tonight, I'll have bare feet and I promise you a sensuous dessert."

"Sorry, Jazz. I'll have to take a rain check, love, I've got a busted wrist - it and some other parts need some massage attention."

"So is Sherri your nurse now?"

"Let's just say she has a healing touch. Oh, by the way do you need me to text you my account details?"

"Yes, do that, Axis," she said churlishly. "Call me tomorrow." She hung up abruptly.

Well, you win some and you lose some when it comes down to dames, some are missing that one special ingredient that presses the right buttons for me, Sherri has it and Jazz doesn't. I suppose Suzie had it too and Rosy certainly did – it makes me wonder if it's a certain vulnerability that attracts me – or is it something deeper that I sense in some women. Certainly it has plenty to do with them wanting me, but that's probably just a macho ego trip. Maybe it's the difference between wanting me for their own pleasure and wanting to share a special moment of intimate ecstasy with me – *share* being the operative word.

The case was pretty much done and dusted I could do no more. It was now a matter of being a creature of habit and changing my ring tone.

In the back of the cab with Sherri on the way back to my apartment I decided it was time for a changing of the guard.

"What are you doing?" Sherri asked.

"I'm changing my ringtone from *Someday Soon* to one of my country favorites *I'll Get By.*"

"Why?"

"I use a different ring tone for each case. Just a quirky habit."

"But you don't have a new case yet."

"Oh, something will pop up soon enough, it always does."

"In the meantime do you want me to stay with you or should I go home?" she said as she moved her hand onto my crotch and felt for Mr. Happy immediately spring into action. "Oh, so that's what you mean by popping up huh?" she giggled.

"You're taking advantage of me while I'm wounded Miss Sherri Sun ... and I love it!"

I told the cabby to let us out at the corner of Goulburn Street.

I checked my bank account at the ATM and both Ty and

Jazz had paid up, it was healthiest my account had ever looked. That called for celebration so I bought a vintage bottle of JD No. 27 Gold Tennessee Whiskey from the liquor store. Normally I wouldn't spend that much money on booze but hell, this was a special occasion, and besides, it was guaranteed to dull the pain in my wrist – like my old Dad used so say about whiskey: *a little medicine goes a long way.*

~ ~ ~

There wasn't a drop left of the JD No. 27 when I tried to drain it into my cup of coffee the next morning – we'd certainly given it a nudge. My wrist-brace had me making a mockery of the effort to put two slices of bread into the toaster. Sherri was still asleep – my phone rang and at first I didn't recognize the ring tone. I searched through the pile of clothes on the living room floor and found it just before it went to message bank. It was Rick, he and Parker had been up all night interrogating Grant Lee and in the end they got a confession: he'd admitted to being the Dragon Head of the Sydney chapter of Sun Yee On ... and for my peace of mind, they determined that Fatty Tung had come to Sydney of his own volition to get square with me for having nailed his mate Soy Ling Chu. They had taken my recommendation and Zhong would arrive today to help them with the final interrogation of both Lee Kit Wo and Fang Peng Jian.

Seems my concern that our celebration last night might have been premature was totally unfounded, because now, as far as I was concerned, the case was closed. I rang Ty and Jazz and told them the good news.

About the Author

Gary Keady (aka Canon Doyle) is a writer, producer, director, film editor and composer with a range of credits in television, film, sound recordings and composing. Gary has owned and operated independent record labels and film production companies in several countries. He has worked in executive management and creative positions in media companies in South East Asia, USA and UK. He has created original programming and formats, and has successfully sold his own work around the world. Broadcasters include *Star TV Hong Kong, RPN 9 Philippines, SBS Singapore, Briz 31 Australia.*

Gary wrote and directed the award winning Australian feature film *"Sons of Steel",* and the 52 episode international television series *P-Max.*

Sons of Steel premiered at the Cannes Film Festival in 1989 and later won critical acclaim with official selection at the 7th Brussels International Festival of Fantastic Film.

NewPulpPress.com
or AbsolutelyAmazingEbooks.com

www.ingramcontent.com/pod-product-compliance
Lightning Source LLC
Chambersburg PA
CBHW060537260626
47161CB00003B/933